PACESETTERS

YOU NEVER KNOW

HELEN OVBIAGELE

First published 1982 By Macmillan Education

Reprint NEOBOOKS © 2025

ISBN: 979-8-89693-055-6

CONTENTS

Macmillan Pacesetters

All the novels in the **Macmillan Pacesetters** series deal with contemporary issues and problems in a way that is particularly designed to interest **young adults**, although the stories are such that they will appeal to all ages.

Titles in the series

Director! **Agbo Areo**

The Smugglers **Kalu Okpi**

The Undesirable Element **Christmas in the City Afari Assan**

Felicia **Rosina Umelo**

The Betrayer **Sam Adewoye**

The Hopeful Lovers **Agbo Areo**

The Delinquent **Mohammed Sule**

The Worshippers **Victor Thorpe**

On the Road **Kalu Okpi**

Too Cold for Comfort **Jide Oguntuoye**

For Mbatha and Rabeka **David Maillu**

The Instrument **Victor Thorpe**

The Wages of Sin **Ibe Oparandu**

Bloodbath at Lobster Close **Dickson Ighavini**

Evbu My Love **Helen Ovbiagele**

Mark of the Cobra **Valentine Alily**

The Black Temple **Mohmed Tukur Garba**

Stone of Vengeance **Victor Thorpe**

Sisi **Yemi Sikuade**

Death is a Woman **Dickson Ighavini**

Tell Me No More **Senzenjani Lukhele**

State Secret **Hope Dube**

Love on the Rocks **Andrew Sesinyi**

The Equatorial Assignment **David Maillu**

Have Mercy **Joseph Mangut**

The Cyclist **Philip Phil-Ebosie**

Agony in her Voice **Peter Katuliiba**

Naira Power **Buchi Emecheta**

Cross-Fire! **Kalu Okpi**

Angel of Death **Nandi Dlovu**

Chapter 1

Everywhere was relatively **quiet** at the Federal Ministry where **Chibuzor Osaro** worked as Senior Executive Officer. It was mid-morning and, for him, this was the best part of the day, when most people settled down to **serious work** after their long and tedious journey to the office through the heavy Lagos traffic. The first hour at work was breakfast time for most junior workers, who had to leave their houses as early as five o'clock to catch the bus. After lunch some people felt drowsy from the intense heat, while others worked half-heartedly and kept an eye on the clock so that they could dash off on the dot of three-thirty and begin the long battle to get home again.

He finished the report he was writing on the new factory at **Ikot-Ubo** in the Cross River State and sat back in his chair. It had been a lengthy report. He looked at his wristwatch: **ten-forty**. Tawa, his typist, was late again.

He didn't know whether to feel angry or sympathetic. The girl lived far away at **Ajegunle** and had to catch several overcrowded buses to work. She could not leave home very early for fear of being molested at bus stops. He had asked Personnel for a change of typist, but she had tearfully asked him to allow her to continue working for him, as no other section was willing to have her because of her **habitual late-coming**. It would be dismissal for her if he rejected her, she had added. He had been moved, but the situation was very trying. He had to submit the report before the end of the day to **Mr Bwala**, his director, and he could not ask someone in the typing pool to type it since it was confidential stuff. Perhaps **Atewe**, Mr Bwala's personal assistant, might be able to suggest someone.

'Sshsh,' she whispered as he entered her office. 'There's an important meeting going on in there—all the departmental heads.'

'Ah, they are probably just **swigging whisky** and gossiping about the rest of us,' he said, winking at her. He bent and kissed her on the cheek. '**Atewe**, light of my life,' he whispered in her ear. 'You look gorgeous. That dress, that hairdo, that perfume—they are simply out of this world. Every flutter of your eyelashes sends my blood racing and I feel like...'

'Here, Chi, kiss me again.' He obliged. She smelt his breath. 'Hm, you're not drunk. It's too early in the day, perhaps. Er, let me see. Ah, I've got it now. You want me to do something for you, hence the flattery. What's that you're hiding behind you?'

'Atewe, you regard any compliment from me with suspicion. You never allow me to get past first base,' he said, laughing. 'Anyway, it's about this report I have to submit to your boss. Tawa is late again and I cannot use the typing pool. So, what do I do? I promised to submit it today and I dare not go back on my word.'

'You'd better not. In fact, we're doing you a **memo** on the matter now. I was just about to type it out.'

'Well, there you are! May I ask what it says

in the memo?'

'You may not! Wait until you get it.'

'Okay, okay. I'm patient. You're always unkind to me.'

'That's Tawa just going past in the corridor.'

'Allah be praised,' he said, quickly picking up his report. 'Luckily she's a fast and fairly accurate typist, so it might be ready in two hours.'

'It should be. Well, Chi darling, I've got lots of work this morning, so if you don't mind...'

'Are you coming to lunch with me today?'

'No, I don't think so. I've got a very full tray. Lunch with you will mean one solid, idle, though pleasant hour. I'll use the staff canteen. See you later.'

'Righto.' At the door he stopped. 'Atewe, I do mean what I said. You certainly look gorgeous today.'

'Only today? That doesn't boost my ego much.'

'Well, er, you look gorgeous almost every day.'

'That's better. Your face is less hideous today, I must say.'

They both laughed and Chibuzor hurried back to his office.

Atewe was one of the top secretaries in the Ministries. She was about Chibuzor's age and was a **widow** with two children. After a short, hectic love affair with him, they had settled into a **brother/sister relationship**, and he became 'uncle' to her children. Through her job she was acquainted with many top government officials and politicians, and this he had found useful on several occasions when he was in a fix. He liked her a lot. She was like a breath of fresh air to him: kind, uninhibited, and unpretentious. Once, he had toyed with the idea of marrying her and had proposed to her. She burst out laughing and told him gently, '**Chibuzor, precious**, you just don't qualify, not even as runner-up. I like you immensely and you're a wonderful lover, but you're **penniless**. I can't start life again with another "beginner". My husband and I struggled to build up a comfortable life, but just as things were beginning to take off, he began to fritter away our money and finally drank himself to death. I had to start all over again. If I do remarry, it would have to be to a **stinking rich old man** who would pamper me no end. If he kicked the bucket, I would at least be well provided for.'

Tawa excelled herself and the report was ready in an hour. After going through it and making a few corrections, Chibuzor gave it back to her. He went to the window and looked down on **Broad Street** below. It was drizzling slightly and the pre-lunch traffic was rapidly building up. At the junction near Bookshop House, a young naked madman was standing in the middle of the road, obstructing the traffic warden who was directing the traffic. The pair began to argue. Drivers hooted impatiently from all directions and the traffic warden looked round helplessly. Two policemen came to his rescue and led the protesting madman away. Traffic began to flow once more. Chibuzor sighed and turned away from the window. Problems, problems! He felt lighthearted now that the report was ready. He hoped it would be accepted this time. Mr Bwala had rejected it twice without giving any cogent reason, other than that he had found it **inadequate**. He had been at a loss what to add or take away, as he had faithfully reported all he had seen in Ikot-Ubo.

Atewe had told him in confidence that she thought Mr Bwala wanted a **favourable report** on the factory, and had advised him to water down his criticisms. This he had now done. To him, the factory was **sub-standard** and the owner should be made to invest in better machinery and more qualified staff before being allowed to continue production. He could not understand why Mr Bwala, who was normally a very strict and moral person, would want a favourable report on a set-up which he knew to be lousy. Had he too joined the ranks of those who got **kickbacks**? Chibuzor did not believe he had. Perhaps a relation or a political party was involved. Anyway, if his boss wanted a favourable report he would have to comply even though it was against his conscience. After all, the **final decision lay above**. All those principles carefully formulated while still at university hardly worked in real life, where every effort of his seemed to be thwarted by superiors. He had been long enough in the civil service to know that you cannot afford to **cross swords with the decision-makers**. Friends told him it was worse in the private sector. It had been difficult at the beginning as he struggled to stick to his beliefs, but after being transferred rapidly from Ministry to Ministry like a bad coin and having his promotions withheld, he had learned to be more **conciliatory** in his attitude. Only a **revolution** could put paid to corruption. He couldn't do much as an individual. He was glad, however, that he had refused the bulky envelope the administrative manager at Ikot-Ubo had tried to press into his hands as he was leaving. He could do with more money, but **bribes** were definitely out. That would be too much for his conscience.

'It's ready, sir,' said Tawa, coming in with

the report.

'Ah, thank you, Tawa. I'll sign and you'll make four photocopies. Here you are.'

'May I go for lunch downstairs afterwards? It's almost one o'clock.'

'That's right. I must go for lunch too. Look, you'll have to hurry over that lunch of yours as we have lots of documents to be filed away, and more things to be typed. You came in **extremely late** today.'

'I'm very sorry. Two of the buses I took broke down on the way and the third ran into another vehicle. I'm really fed up, sir. If only I could afford to move to a place nearer the office, I would.'

'All right, Tawa, just make an effort to come in early.' He didn't think she tried hard enough.

'I will, sir. I really do try my best. I really do.'

'I'm going down the road for my lunch.'

'Yes. You have some letters. Here they are.'

'Thank you.' One was from his mother who lived in **Ogba**, on the outskirts of Warri. He smiled and put it in his pocket. He would read it while having lunch. Letters from his mother always made good reading, for they contained, amongst other things, titbits about neighbours and the hottest gossip in town, and these were always presented in a **humorous** way.

Later, at the **Coral Restaurant**, he looked at the food placed before him without interest. It was his favourite plate of **pounded yam and vegetable soup**, which was a speciality of the restaurant's, and he had looked forward to it that afternoon, but now the food had turned to **ashes in his mouth**. The reason was the letter from his mother which contained some disturbing news about his twenty-one-year-old sister, **Ivie**, who was married and had just had her second baby girl. Ivie, his mother said, was back with her children at the family house after a bitter quarrel with her husband, **Sola**, over his threat to take a **second wife** because she had produced yet another baby girl. If he had his way, Chibuzor would leave the couple to sort out their own problems, but he knew that wouldn't do. His mother would worry herself sick until things were okay again. He loved his mother and sisters, but this business of being **head of the family** was wearing him out and affecting his work and social life. Since his father died he had had to travel to Ogba frequently to sort out one problem or the other. Nothing was too trivial to be referred to him. He would have to make yet another trip home, but this time he decided he would have to tell his mother that these trips were not very convenient. There would be bruised feelings but they would all be better off in the end.

He sighed, picked up his knife and fork and began to cut a piece of meat. A fly perched on his wrist. He flicked it off.

'Oh, no,' cried a young lady at the next table. She stood up. 'See what you've done! Oh my goodness! What do I do now?'

Chibuzor and the few diners in the restaurant turned to look. The poor lady had been dressed in an immaculate **white linen trouser suit**. She looked smart and attractive, but thanks to Chibuzor the suit was now dotted with the yellowish stains of **palm oil**. The kitchen of the popular Coral Restaurant was always liberal with oil in the soup.

'Oh dear,' cried Chibuzor in consternation. 'Did I do that?' He got up agitatedly and knocked his table over. His food went flying across the room. Luckily there was no other person at his table. Waiters rushed to the rescue. The proprietress came out of her office and clucked sympathetically while mentally calculating how much extra she could subtly shove on Chibuzor's bill to cover broken plates and glass. He was a regular customer there but still, **business was business**.

'The trouble with Mr Osaro,' said the proprietress to the lady in white as she led her to the washroom to see what could be done with the trouser suit, 'is that he is **too large**. He is a nice and likeable young man but he sows destruction everywhere with almost every movement he makes. If there's a single chair in a large room he is sure to trip over it. If there isn't, he will trip over his toe. That's why we try as much as possible to put him at a table by himself, except, of course, when he has guests.'

The other lady giggled. 'So, he's a regular customer of yours?'

'Yes. He's been coming here for about four years now. He works for the Federal Ministry across the road.'

'I work nearby too, but this is my first time here. Dear me, I don't think this will come off now.'

'I don't think so either,' sympathised the proprietress. 'You'll have to have it **dry-cleaned**.'

'And I have a meeting at two o'clock.'

'You can't go like this. If you don't live far away, you could go home and change; otherwise you could buy something cheap at **Tinubu Square** to tide you over. Say, a **tie-and-dye T-shirt and skirt** for about **ten naira**. I can send one of my girls to buy them for you.'

'No, thank you. I think I'll go home. I live in Ikoyi.'

'There's no problem then. It's just about a fifteen minute' drive away.'

'I've no car. I hope I'll get a taxi quickly. This meeting is very important.'

'If Mr Osaro's car is on the road today, I'm sure he'll be only too glad to oblige.'

'He might have left already.'

'I doubt it. He's too much of a gentleman to run away like that.'

'Can I go into the street like this? Not that I have a choice.'

'Never mind, people won't stare too much.'

Chibuzor was hovering around when they came back into the dining room.

'I can see that it did not come off,' he said on seeing them. 'Can I drive you home to change?' he offered half-heartedly. 'Or would you rather I put you in a taxi?'

'Please drive me home. I live at **Lugard**

Road in Ikoyi.'

'It's my lucky day. That's not far.' He had so much work on his desk.

'Please could we go quickly?' said the lady urgently. 'I've an appointment at two. I cannot afford to be late.'

'Half a minute, please. They are preparing the bills.'

'Yes, I must settle mine too.'

'No, I'll see to that. I'm terribly sorry I ruined your suit and your lunch.'

'I hadn't started lunch yet. I had only had a bottle of coca-cola.'

He settled the bills and they left.

The traffic was light, and very shortly they were at her house and she let herself in while he waited in the car.

'Hello, Mum,' she called out. 'Where are you?'

'Here, **Yetunde**, in the kitchen. Home for lunch? Cancelled your meeting?'

'No. You were right, Mum,' she said, giving her mother a peck on the cheek. 'I should not have worn the white suit.'

Mrs Adebayo straightened up from where she had been putting dough into the oven. She adjusted her glasses and looked at her daughter.

'What happened? Someone splashed mud on you? The rainy season is no time for white clothes. Let me see. We can get it off easily,' she said, moving closer. 'Oh, it's an **oil stain**!'

'Yes, Mum.' Briefly, she told her what had happened, and dashed upstairs to change.

'Shall I ask the young man in?' her mother called after her.

'No, Mum. There's no time for such courtesy. I'm in a hurry. Where's Dad?'

'He's gone for a round of golf at his Club. Shall I wrap up some **meat pies** for you? I've made some to take to the **Motherless Babies' Home** in the evening.'

'Oh yes. It's a Wednesday, isn't it?'

'Yes, dear.' Every Wednesday she baked for one charity organisation or the other. Twice a week she spent four hours doing voluntary work at **Maroko Maternity Home**. She was a retired midwife.

'Just two meat pies will do, Mum,' said Yetunde, coming into the kitchen. She had changed into a smart brown frock.

'That was quick. You look lovely. Here are the meat pies, and here are some **fairy cakes** for the young man who was kind enough to bring you all the way home.'

'Mum, what for? Not after ruining my clothes. I ought to take him to court or something. The **clumsy oaf**. He has not even offered to pay for cleaning my suit.'

'Never mind, dear, it was a mistake. Give the cakes to him.'

'All right, if you say so. He looks nice, though. You ought to see him. He's about **ten feet tall**, and bearded too. His head actually touches the roof of his car. He should have an operation for height reduction. He's enough to give a child **nightmares**.'

'Yetunde!' exclaimed her mother.

'What's the time? I must dash, Mum. See you later.'

Chibuzor was surprised when Yetunde gave him the cakes.

'That's very kind of your mother. Is she always this generous to strangers she has not even met?'

'Not always, but she tries her best.'

'By the way, we've not introduced ourselves. I'm **Chibuzor Osaro**. I work for the Federal Ministry at Broad Street.'

'It's nice to meet you. I'm **Yetunde Adebayo**. I'm an artist with **Owens International** at the Marina.'

'It's a pleasure meeting you. Do you come often to the Coral Restaurant? I've never seen you there.'

'I usually go home for lunch. Besides, I've only been with the company for six months.'

'I see.'

Chibuzor was thoughtful as he drove Yetunde back to her office. He dropped her on the pavement outside, and didn't look back as he drove away.

Chibuzor's trip to Warri that weekend turned out to be **unnecessary**, as he was told when he got to Sola's house that he and Ivie had taken the children to an amusement park. Well, this was welcome news, as they would not have been going out together if they were still at war. He later drove down to **Ogba** to see his mother, who told him that Sola had come for his family shortly after she had posted the letter. She had forgotten to write another letter informing him that the quarrel was over, and that there was no more talk of a second wife. Chibuzor smiled. He doubted if Sola would ever carry out his threat even if they had twenty daughters for, apart from being crazy about his wife, he was scared of quarrels in the home; and this he would

surely have if he took a second wife.
However, it was **cruel** of him to keep such a
cloud hanging over Ivie's head.

Mrs Osaro's main problem since the death
of her husband had been **loneliness**,
particularly now that the youngest daughter
was away in a boarding school. Chibuzor
was aware of this, so, on this trip, he
suggested to her that she should come and
live with him for a while in Lagos. She
thanked him but **declined**, saying that Ogba
was dear to her as it held happy memories
of her life with her late husband. Besides,
all her friends lived there and she wanted to
be near her daughters. In the end, it was
decided that she should come out of
retirement and **go back to work**. The idea
appealed to her enormously and, before
Chibuzor left the next day, they had both
contacted one or two people about the
matter. He went back to Lagos
lighthearted, for he knew that once his
mother found something to occupy her time,
she was capable of tackling most problems
and would not ask him to come to Ogba for
every minor incident.

Some time later, he and Atewe were having lunch one day at the Coral Restaurant when Yetunde came in with two other ladies. As they passed by their table she nodded at him. He half rose, almost upset the table, and sat down again.

'Steady now, Chibuzor,' said Atewe. 'Do you want the waiter?'

'No, no, I don't,' then in an excited low voice, 'It's **her**.'

'Her, who?' asked Atewe, looking round.

'The lady I told you about. The one whose suit I stained here the other day. She works with Owens International.'

'She's here today? The lady of your dreams? Where is she?'

'Over there in the corner. She's with two other ladies. Don't stare so hard at them, Atewe.'

'I'm sorry,' she laughed. 'I thought you wanted me to look at them. Which is she?'

'The best of the three. The prettiest.'

'Ah, the plump one with a headtie and a squint?'

'No, she's a washout. It's the dark slim one in a **cream blouse**. There! She's looking this way and smiling.' He waved and Yetunde waved back.

'She's pretty,' conceded Atewe. 'What's her name?'

'I don't know, or rather, I've forgotten. I was a little upset the day we met and my mind went blank afterwards—only her face stuck. I felt such a fool when I called at her office and the receptionist asked me to describe her. I tried to, and the silly girl could not stop giggling. Very unnerving.'

'Why didn't you call at her house since you know where she lives?'

'I did, but the guard at the gate pretended he understood neither English nor any Nigerian language. It was so **frustrating**.'

'Poor you! How you've suffered! Well, you've found her again and the **ball is now in your court**.'

'True, but what do I say to her? How do I get her to go out with me?'

'Don't be funny, Chibuzor. This is unlike you. You're usually a **fast worker** as far as girls are concerned.'

'Yes, but this time I'm a little scared she might refuse to go out with me. She might think I'm just another guy, out for fun.'

She laughed. 'Well, aren't you? However, there are other girls you could ask out if she refuses.'

'No, there aren't. At least not when someone like her is around.'

'Ha! Sorry, I'll have to leave you behind now. I've some things to buy at Tinubu.'

'Hey, Atewe, don't abandon me.'

'You certainly don't need me hanging around,' she teased. 'It might spoil things. Come and tell me all the details later. See you!' She placed a hand on his shoulder. 'Boy, you're trembling slightly. It must be a serious matter.' She laughed again and left.

His plates were cleared away and he ordered another bottle of beer to while away the time while Yetunde and her friends finished their meal.

As they passed by his table on their way out he got up. 'Good afternoon, Miss er... er,' he said to Yetunde as her friends moved off.

'Good afternoon, Mr Osaro,' she replied, smiling.

He felt awkward at not remembering her name. 'I'm sorry, I've no head for names. Forgive me.'

'You're forgiven. The name is **Yetunde Adebayo**.'

'So it is. I called at your office once to find out if, er, er, dry-cleaning got those stains off your clothes.'

'How thoughtful of you. What happened? Was I out?'

'I couldn't say. The receptionist was most unco-operative.'

'That was a pity. However, most of the

stains came off. Further dry-cleaning might get it all off.'

'I'm sorry.'

'That's all right.'

'May I take you out some time, say, to the pictures or for a drink?'

'Fine. I'd love that.'

'Tonight?' he asked eagerly.

'No, not tonight. I've a date. **Saturday**, maybe.'

'Five days away!' he said, a bit disappointed.

'Okay.'

She had no date lined up for that night but it was her policy never to make things very easy for men who were eager to date her. Not at the outset, at any rate. She did not intend to keep the Saturday night date either. The **suspense** would do the man some good. If he was really keen, he would call again. She had liked him the day they met and had hoped that they would see more of each other.

When they began going out together they made an interesting pair; Chibuzor, twenty-nine, tall, **burly** and heavily **bearded**; Yetunde, twenty-two, of average height, very slim and delicate looking. On his part, it was all **feverish love** which, unlike past associations with girls, refused to die out. She was more cautious in her feelings, although she knew she was falling in love with him more and more. He was not exactly her type. She was **dreamy** whereas he was more **down-to-earth**.

There were objections to the relationship from **Tola** and **Tricia**, her bosom friends, with whom she had been to the same grammar school and university. They felt she had **lowered her standards** and theirs by accepting someone like him. His appearance was nothing to write home about, they claimed, but his most hideous offence was that he was a **penniless civil servant**. This the girls could not forgive. They told her that if she wanted a civil servant as a boyfriend, she could at least have gone in for someone at the very top.

They became even more worried when she dropped all other dates to concentrate on Chibuzor. She was called to Tricia's flat for a **serious talk**. She was very unhappy that her boyfriend was not acceptable to her friends, for they had all been very close. Now, however, she was in love and wanted to have her own way. This attitude angered the other two.

'Now, **Tunde**,' said Tricia, who at twenty-five was the oldest of the three. 'You've been going out steadily with Mr Osaro for the past four months. We're surprised—no, shocked—that instead of dropping this man, since he falls short of our standards, your association with him has become more intense. Could you explain, please?'

'I love him.'

'Love whom?' asked Tricia with disdain. 'You can't love him. The man looks like a **gorilla**.'

'He doesn't,' retorted Yetunde.

'I'm sorry, but he does.'

'Here,' said Tola, 'Let's be fair. Some people might find him good looking. One man's meat is another man's poison. Anyway, what he looks like is not our major objection.'

'That's true,' said Tricia. 'Our main objection is that he's a penniless **low-grade officer**.'

'He's not a low-grade officer. He's a **Senior Executive Officer**.'

'That's **salary level 10**, I think, in the Civil Service: ₦ 5000 plus to ₦ 6000 plus. Ridiculous!

'How can he take you out to posh places on that? Are you going to change your lifestyle now? And all because of a man? It's not worth it.'

'He may not have much money, but I'm quite happy with him. In fact, he's just proposed to me.' He hadn't yet, but he would. She could feel it, and when he did she was going to accept without **hesitation**.

'Has he now?' asked Tola. 'I hope you had the sense to turn him down.'

'I did nothing of the sort. I accepted.'

'You did what?' exclaimed both girls, staring at her in amazement.

'You're pulling our legs,' said Tricia. 'You wouldn't do such a thing. You, who love expensive things and the company of important people. The marriage won't last a month, I can assure you.'

'It will last much longer than that. It will last a long time. We love each other. Having lots of money is no longer a big thing with me. I'm a changed person.'

The other two laughed scornfully.

'We've heard that one before,' said Tricia. 'Tola here has told you and me that several times in the past, but we talked sense into her.'

'Yes, but she couldn't have been so deeply in love as I am at the moment, otherwise she wouldn't have listened to us.'

'Hm,' said Tola. 'Could the man have made some **juju** on her or what?'

'Nonsense, Tola,' said Tricia. 'We don't really believe in that, do we? She's just being stubborn. Look, Tunde, we're concerned about you and your future. We regard one another as sisters and what hurts one hurts the others. Tola and I cannot allow you to contract an **alliance** we know will fail. At least not without warning you. You've not been used to counting pennies, right from your childhood.'

'We won't be counting pennies. I've a good job, remember?'

'Yes, but a man should be capable of looking after his family comfortably. You'll spend all your time pushing his broken-down vehicle to and from work. I understand he drives a battered **Volkswagen Beetle**.'

'You'll age in no time,' said Tola, 'going from stall to stall in the market looking for **bargains**.'

'You won't be able to dress in the style you're accustomed to, and when the children come, things will be worse. You won't be able to afford to stop working in order to look after them. You'll have to get a **nanny** or drag the poor things to a **day care centre** every day.'

'Holidays, of course, are ruled out.'

'The man probably has a lot of relations who are dependent on his salary. You'll live like **paupers**.'

'And since you're not used to such a life, the quarrels will start and...'

Yetunde put her fingers to her ears. 'It wouldn't matter, it wouldn't matter,' she said hotly, trying desperately to blot out the image of what they were saying.

'Anyway, what do your parents say about the association?' asked Tricia.

'My mother has met him and likes him.'

'Is that so? Very strange. What about papa?'

'He hasn't met Chibuzor yet.'

'That's all right, then. He won't be accepted. His looks will disqualify him. Your father can't stand **ugly people**.'

'I will still marry him even if my father disapproves.'

'Rubbish!' said the girls.

'You wouldn't dare,' said Tricia. 'Yours is a very **closely knit family**. You'll be afraid of being **disowned**.'

'Look,' said Yetunde, getting angry and fed up with the probe. They were talking to her as if she were **mentally retarded**. They probably meant well, but she wished she could be left alone. Her head throbbed. 'Close friends or no close friends, please keep your opinions to yourselves. If you really are fond of me, you would be glad for me. It's my life, after all. I've this uneasy feeling that you're **jealous** of my close relationship with Chibuzor.'

'What?' exclaimed Tricia. 'Jealous of you! Why on earth should I be?'

'She's gone crazy,' said Tola. 'Leave her alone.'

'No, I won't. Tunde, did you say I'm jealous of you?'

'Yes,' retorted Yetunde. She was tired and the hammer in her head was pounding faster. 'You especially. You're afraid of ending up on the **shelf**. There's no marriage proposal on your horizon, so you're jealous because I'm getting serious with someone.'

'What? Please **get out of my flat!** Right now.'

'No, Tricia, no,' said Tola, getting in between the two. 'Yetunde, say you're sorry.'

'I won't. What have I done wrong? She's been unnecessarily bitter about the whole thing.'

'Get out or I'll **murder you** this instant.'

'I'll go with pleasure.' She made for the door.

'Don't ever show your face here again.'

Yetunde was already out of the flat. That was the **end of the trio's friendship**.

'What are you thinking of, Yetunde, my precious?' Chibuzor asked her one evening in his flat. 'Come into my arms. You look sad. What's the matter, sweetheart?'

She went to him.

'I was thinking of our love.'

'Oh,' he said, not quite knowing what to say in response. Being in love with Yetunde and being loved by her was a whole new experience for him. Perhaps it was the **artist** in her. Whatever it was, it made him feel good. He loved her so much.

He drew her close. 'What were you thinking about our love, darling?' He hoped the question didn't sound as silly to her as it did to him. If anyone had told him he would ever talk to any lady in that fashion, he would have laughed his head off. Who had time for such **frivolity**?

She laid her head on his shoulder. 'I'm wondering if we'll still be in love like this, say, in about **thirty years' time**.'

'If we're both alive, why not? My love for you will always be as intense as this. I love you, Yetunde.'

'Chi, you make me feel so loved. I'm so happy.' Her eyes glistened with tears.

'Why the tears?'

'You talked about being alive. What about if one of us should die? How will the other take it?'

'Ah, don't worry about that, sweetheart. We shall die at the **same time**. When you're ready, just let me know, and I shall say, "Righto lady, lead the way. Let's go." Very simple really.'

They both laughed and kissed.

Mrs Adebayo had been used to seeing her daughter fall in and out of love frequently, but she had never seen her looking so happy and content. Chibuzor was introduced to her, and gradually she came to like him. **Appearances are deceptive**, and beneath all the frightening exterior lay a kind heart which was very fond of her daughter. She was a bit apprehensive about what her husband's reaction to the young man would be. He categorised people into good or bad according to their looks. '**Ugly people do ugly things**', he used to say. If a good-looking person committed the most hideous crime, he was prepared to forgive him, whereas nothing an ugly person did ever impressed him. She fervently hoped that Chibuzor would be accepted by her husband, for she could not see Yetunde giving him up if he were rejected. She would marry him even if she hadn't planned to, just for the **hell of it**. All hell would break loose in the house if the daughter disobeyed father, and she loved peace around her. Perhaps Chibuzor's nice manners would see him through. She decided to invite him for dinner so he could be introduced to the family. The sooner they all knew where they stood, the better.

That Saturday, after preparing dinner with the help of Yetunde and **Marcel**, the househelp, she sat down with her husband to watch the television. Yetunde was upstairs getting ready. The doorbell went, and as Marcel was in his room, **Mr Adebayo** went to answer it. As usual, he first looked through the window to see who it was. He tiptoed back to his wife without opening the door, and whispered.

'There's **something** at the door,' he said, with comical round eyes.

'Something?' asked his wife, puzzled.

'When I say something, I mean an **animal**. Sort of.'

'An animal, **Wole**?'

'Well, a person, if you like,' he admitted grudgingly. 'Big, all beard. Like a **gorilla**.'

'A gorilla! Wole!' said his wife reproachfully. 'That will be Yetunde's young man. Nice boy. They are very much in love. I told you he was coming to dinner.'

'That thing! Yetunde's young man!' he cried in horror, looking at a photograph of his elder daughter which hung on the wall. *The oval face, the high forehead, the aquiline nose, and delicate mouth, all my own,* he thought proudly. *And that thing at the door! Heavens!*

'Who invited him for dinner?' he asked, outraged. 'No one ever tells me anything in this house. No one asks my opinion. Decisions are taken over my head as if I'm no longer **head of this family**. I'm not surprised. A house full of women.'

'Calm down darling,' said his wife gently. 'You know you're very much the active head of this family. I did tell you Yetunde's young man was coming to dinner. You said, "Fine."'

'Yes, but you said a friend of hers.'

'Well, he's a friend of hers, Wole.'

'I suppose so. But I ought to have been warned about what he looked like.'

'Why?'

'If I'm to spend the evening staring into a face like a **bandit's** across my dining table, I have a right to know so that I can be ready with my **indigestion tablets** in my pocket.'

'Wole,' said his wife, laughing. 'You do like to exaggerate. Let the young man in.'

The doorbell went again.

'Coming,' called Yetunde, rushing down the stairs. 'Mum, Dad, that must be Chibuzor. I'll open the door.'

'I must say his name is most apt,' said Mr Adebayo when his daughter was out of earshot. '**Chimpanzee**! The parents couldn't have chosen a more appropriate name!'

'It's **Chibuzor**, Wole, and please be nice to him. He's very polite and pleasant when you get to know him. Well-bred, too. His parents were school teachers.'

'Hm! You said they are in love?'

'Yes.'

'I'm sure it will blow over like all the others. I don't want grandchildren I can't take to the zoo for fear people will mistake them for **little gorillas**.'

'They are coming,' whispered his wife. 'They might hear you. Stop scowling.'

'Why should I? This is my house and Yetunde is my daughter. The man should try his best to please me and win me over.' Whereupon he sat down, crossed his legs, and assumed a **haughty expression**.

Later that night when they were alone, Mrs Adebayo asked her husband what he thought of Chibuzor.

'He seems all right,' he said reluctantly. 'At least he had the good sense to join the **Civil Service**. Most of our young men and women are so **money-minded** these days that they won't serve their government because of the poor pay. Many opt for the private sector.'

'They need the money for their lifestyle. Not everyone can pinch and stretch a **kobo** like we used to. I didn't enjoy it.'

'Maybe not, but I got a lot of satisfaction from serving the government. However, Chi,

Chip, what's his name, seems like an intelligent fellow. He has nice manners, too. Oh well, we'll see. I suppose it isn't his fault he looks the way he does.'

His wife laughed. 'Don't be silly. Chibuzor is a very attractive young man. Very **masculine**. Women would feel protected with him around.'

'Hm! Watch it, girl,' said her husband, **baring his teeth**.

Chapter 2

Yetunde and Chibuzor were married **eighteen months later** and they moved into a lovely flat in **Oshodi** which they did up to their taste. Although she missed the **low-density area** she had lived in most of her life, Yetunde tried hard to adjust and keep a happy home. She felt she could live anywhere so long as she was with her husband, but it was the **heavy traffic** which put a lot of strain on her.

'Now you know how the **other half lives**,' teased Chibuzor one night when they both collapsed into their chairs after spending **three hours** in traffic in a heavy downpour.

'How do people survive in a town like this, living such a life? Two hours to get to work in the morning and two hours to get back, moving at a snail's speed.'

'That's if you're lucky and have transport of your own.'

'And you have to set out again the next morning.'

'Of course. If you set out too early, you're attacked by **armed robbers**; too late, and you're late for work.'

'I adore this flat, but it would be nice living a bit closer to where we both work,' she said wistfully.

'True, precious, but getting accommodation to suit both one's needs and pocket is a **big problem** in this country.'

'I know.' She snuggled close to him. 'Chi, couldn't we take up Dad's offer?'

'Dad's offer?' he said lightly. 'What was it?'

'That we live with them in Ikoyi until we get something suitable or the Ministry gives you a flat over there.'

'Isn't this flat suitable? Isn't the neighbourhood good enough?' he said, his voice rising.

'You know how much I love this flat, but the distance to town is too much and since my sister **Peju** is away at school and, anyway, there are extra rooms...?'

'It's out of the question, darling. I know your parents are kind, but it is **unAfrican** for a man to house his family under the roof of his **parents-in-law**. Call it **male pride** if you like. Why, it would seem as if I'm unable to look after my family. My father would turn in his grave at such a thought. I'm sure your parents, too, don't seriously expect me to take up the offer.'

'Yes, but...'

'Ssh, ssh, Yetunde,' he said, grinning and placing a finger on her lips. 'We'll manage. Other families do. If we had our own house over here, we would not refuse to live in it simply because it was a long way from our offices. Many of my colleagues live on the outskirts of Lagos and they can still cope.'

'True. We'll survive, I suppose.'

'That's the spirit. Come on, I'm starving. Let's rustle up something.'

When their first baby was on the way, they decided that Yetunde should give up her job with the advertising company and find something less strenuous and nearer the house. She took a job as an **Art teacher** in a Technical College in Oshodi. The **remuneration** was low compared with what she used to earn, but she was a happier and more relaxed person. Chibuzor was happy too, although he missed his wife's company to and from work, it was nice to come home to a tidy flat, a hot meal, and a contented wife.

The baby was given the name **Oghogho** by Chibuzor's mother, and Atewe was one of the godmothers. Mr Adebayo had now almost overcome his prejudice against his son-in-law's appearance and had even developed some affection and respect for him. He was proud of his progress in the Civil Service. In a way, they were alike—stubborn, hard-working, and ambitious. When his first granddaughter turned out to be a pretty little thing, he was overjoyed, and at the first sight of her he had remarked what a clever girl she was. 'You don't have to look far to see where she gets her fantastic good looks. **From me**, of course.' The baby's parents smiled indulgently.

During the next ten years, the Osaros had three more children: **Efe, Uyi, and Nohowa.** Nothing had changed in the relationship between the couple as they were still very fond of each other, and the children drew them even closer together. Although she had a househelp, Yetunde still worked as a teacher and was a devoted wife and mother. Meanwhile, Chibuzor had made the rounds of several more Ministries and after several promotions became **Director** in one of the Federal Ministries at the **Federal Government Secretariat** and was given a house in **Ikoyi**.

Although he enjoyed his job and position, he sometimes wished he had taken up a more lucrative job in the private sector and been able to keep his family in more comfort. It would be nice to be able to take his wife and children for a **holiday abroad** every year, get a third car and a driver for the kids, and build a house. He knew that with his qualifications and experience there would be no problem getting a lucrative position, but he enjoyed working for the government. It made him feel important that he could help take a decision which could in one way or the other affect the **economy of his country**. He knew too that he could make good money, as some of his colleagues did, by **turning a blind eye** while a company flouted some regulation laid down by the government. Sometimes he did wonder if he was not being foolish to keep on refusing these bribes. After all, some of the favours asked for were quite **harmless**, even though they were forbidden.

'It isn't worth it, my boy,' said his father-in-law one day during one of their conversations. 'There was a time during my service when I had a lot of say in the award of contracts. Big **tips** were offered and it was difficult to keep on refusing them, but I did. It was my wife's father who made some money. He was offered money by a desperate bidder in return for talking me into awarding him a big contract. The old man accepted the money and stuck to it like glue, although he was quite aware that he could not help the man.'

'So what did the man do?'

'Nothing. My father-in-law refused to return the money, saying that he had fulfilled his assignment which was to talk to me about giving the contract to the man. He said he never promised the man would get it.'

'Tough old man.'

'One of the toughest. That was how he made his pile. He was a **ruthless businessman**. When the man kept bothering him to return the money, he sent some hefty men round to warn him to keep off or things would start happening to him. The man was scared.'

'Poor man.'

'He's struck it rich since then and is doing well. The funny thing is, he could have got the contract easily because his was a good and reputable company, but I decided not to give it to him when the old man tried to persuade me to. He did not disclose that he

had been given some money. I only guessed.
The truth came out later.'

'You must have been hated by many
frustrated people.'

'Probably. One thing was certain;
construction companies who got my
contracts made sure they **delivered the
goods**. Yessir! I dictated the tune. No
shoddy work for me. That was why I
retired as a poor man. Junior officers in my
department built fabulous houses. I have
only just finished paying for the only house
I own.'

'It's a lovely house, sir.'

'Thank you. What would I want with several
houses when so many people in this country
are **destitute** and sleep under the bridges?'

'Precisely. You can only sleep in one room at
any given time.'

'True, and later when there are accusations
and **probes**, imagine how embarrassing it
would be for you and your family if it was
proved that you had been dishonest. Some

of the property would be seized by the government. The disgrace would be enough to send a man to an **early grave**.'

Yetunde was shopping at the **Uwa Departmental Stores** one Saturday morning when she ran into **Inyang**, an old classmate of hers at the **Ahmadu Bello University**.

'Yetunde!' someone called excitedly as she stood in the queue at a checkout counter.

'Inyang,' she exclaimed on recognising the attractive and elegantly dressed lady. They had not seen each other since they left **Zaria** many years before. They hugged and went upstairs to the restaurant. Yetunde was amazed at the **transformation** in Inyang, who had been regarded as the ugliest girl in their class. She had hardly any dates and all the other girls, including Yetunde, looked down on her and particularly on her **shabby way of dressing**. Her good point was that she was the joy of every teacher—the ideal student. And now, here was this lovely lady who looked at least five years younger than her age. Yetunde became very **self-conscious** about her **plump figure** and

dowdy dress. Something Tricia and Tola had said about 'ageing in no time due to financial strain' flitted across her mind. She sat up straight in her chair and tried to look bright and sophisticated. She stole a glance at her reflection in the window. Lovely face still, but something would have to be done urgently about the slightly visible **double chin**; a face massage or something, then exercise and a strict diet. She knew all the **ropes**; it was just the **willpower**.

The ladies smiled at each other after ordering their drinks. Yetunde made sure she ordered **soda water**. 'The strict diet starts now,' she told herself firmly. They exchanged news of old friends and then Inyang asked Yetunde about herself.

'I'm teaching at the moment. Actually, I've been teaching for about twelve or thirteen years now.'

'Really? I thought you were working with an advertising company. Someone told me that.'

'Yes, that was before the children started coming. I wanted to have more time for them and the home. You know how difficult it is to get **househelps** these days, even if you can afford the high wages.'

'That's true.'

'So, somehow, I just got stuck with teaching and stayed. I enjoy it, though. It is particularly rewarding when you run into **ex-pupils** who've done well in life.'

'I know. I taught for three years myself and I thoroughly enjoyed it, although I must say that children do not seem to be keen on learning these days.'

'A great number of them, yes. They simply don't **give a damn**.'

'What's your married name?'

'Osaro.'

'How many children?'

'Four. A girl and three boys.'

'You've not done badly. You look content. Are you happy?'

'Yes, very happy. My husband is quite reasonable, thank goodness. He's a civil servant and of course not rich, but we get on quite well. Er, what about you? Are you married?'

'Yes, I'm **Mrs Akpan**. My husband is a chartered accountant. He set up a company with a friend of his. They are doing fairly well.'

'Any children?' asked Yetunde. *Here's where I score a point,* she told herself as she thought smugly of her lovely kids and eyed the other's shapely figure.

'I have a large family,' said Inyang, half-apologetically. **'Five children.'**

'Five children! Then please tell me how you are able to have such a trim figure still, and have time to look so lovely. I'm always looking harassed. Or maybe they don't live with you.'

'Oh, they do. I wouldn't want someone else to raise my children for me. I have a househelp but, most important of all, I make the children look after themselves and help around the house. The youngest is six. As for my figure, well, thanks for saying something nice about it. I eat sensibly and play lots of **squash** at the weekend. I put on weight easily. I was very fat after my last baby. I had to go to that popular **health farm** at **Isale-Eko**. It cost me a fortune and it was hard work, but I emerged as a new woman.'

'I don't think I can afford that.'

'It's **sinfully expensive**. The thought of going there again and paying all that money puts me off my food and makes me keep my weight the way it is.'

'It would me, too,' laughed Yetunde. 'Do you work?'

'At the moment, no. I'm trying to set up my own business—an **art shop**. I worked with my husband for several years.'

'Did you like it? I wouldn't.'

'I didn't mind, but things did not work out as tension in the house was carried on to the office, so we decided that I should do something else. Now **John** and I enjoy a more cordial relationship.'

'Opening an art shop is a brave venture. Do you have the capital?'

'I could only put up half of it. I'm looking for a **partner**, actually.'

'You'll get one. Where's the shop?'

'At the **Tafawa Balewa Square**. I've been allocated three large rooms.'

'What will be your line? Just paintings?'

'No, that wouldn't fetch much. What I have in mind is a sort of **gift shop**—paintings, sculpture, bronze work, local **tie-and-dye** stuff, cards, and the rest of it. It would involve a lot of travelling and attending exhibitions.'

'Sounds exciting. I'm sure you'll make a success of it.'

'I feel so too. Thanks.'

That evening Yetunde stood in front of her mirror and took a critical look at herself. **Thirty-seven**, mother of four, teacher, **flabby** and unattractive, and leading a dull and uneventful life. She thought of Inyang again with some **envy**. Actually, she had been pretty content with her life until the encounter that morning. The meeting had jolted her into realising that she had allowed herself to get into a **rut**. She must do something about it and get more **zip** out of life before she becomes **senile**. She would have to change jobs; probably go back to advertising or something equally challenging. It would mean long hours away from her family, but she was sure she could reorganise things so that no one suffered. **Nohowa**, the youngest child, was five, and she had a good nanny and housekeeper in **Martine**.

She lost **half a stone** in three months, and was very pleased when the children noticed it and told her that her dresses were now too big for her. She bought some new clothes to celebrate and, encouraged by her new look, she began to think seriously of changing jobs. She contacted her old firm. They were delighted to hear from her, but had no opening yet. Perhaps in **six months' time**. She went for some interviews and there were promises but nothing came out of them. She was disappointed and she moaned to her husband who did not think she had a problem.

'Why the bother? You have a good job you enjoy, and the pay is not bad for a housewife.'

'I don't enjoy teaching any more. I've told you so several times. I need a change. Besides, the pay is poor.'

'It's okay. We are not rich, but we are not poor either.'

'I know, but we could be a bit more comfortable and be able to afford **little extras**.'

'Who's complaining? Certainly not me or the children. I used to wish I had more money to lavish on my family like some of my friends, but I realise that being happy is more important—happy in your job, in your family, in...'

'But are we happy together as man and wife?' she asked, getting up from her chair and going to the window.

He was shocked by her utterance. 'Yetunde, what did you say?'

'I asked if we are happy together. You hardly notice me any more.'

'What do you mean by that?' He went to her and made her face him. 'What is it, precious? What's bothering you? It can't be the job?'

She pushed him away. 'Leave me alone. You hardly look at me these days. What do you care? I've been starving myself to death for the past four months so as to lose weight and look pretty for you, but you pretended not to notice. Only this morning the children remarked how nice I look now I'm slimmer. When did you last pay me any compliment? You don't love me any more. Do I deserve such treatment?' She began to **sob**.

'Don't cry, darling,' he said, pulling her into his arms. 'I'm sorry if I've not been as lavish with my compliments as I used to be, but that does not mean that I now love you less. I just thought, well, you always look attractive, so why labour the point? As for your being plump, perhaps you did put on a bit of weight after having our children, but that was to be expected. If you're pleased now that you're shedding it, fine. However, to me you're still the girl I fell in love with and I find you as pretty as the first time I saw you.'

'Oh, Chibuzor,' she said softly, burying her face in his chest.

'I love you, Yetunde.'

'I love you, too, Chi.'

Later that night as his wife slept in his arms, Chibuzor stared into the dark, thinking. Were things beginning to go wrong with their marriage? Why should Yetunde at this stage be whining and moaning about compliments and care? She ought to know that she was well loved.

Why, he had not had a **single affair** in their **sixteen years of marriage**. To him, that was commendable, considering how his friends indulged in **extra-marital affairs**. He found other women attractive, certainly, but he had never felt the urge to make love to them. This was strange because he had been one of the foremost **playboys on the campus** during his days at the **University of Nigeria, Nsukka**. His wife's needs matched his and he still found her exciting. Besides, he had been busy all these years trying to get to the top in his career and such diversions were out. What was the matter with her? Was she getting bored with being married to him? Maybe he ought to have remarked on her new sleek look and encouraged her, but actually he preferred her slightly plump. She was more **cuddly** that way. **Women!** You could never fully understand them. Could it be the approach of the **menopause**? She was too young for that. He tried to recall what friends had said about the menopause but couldn't. And he, Chibuzor, what was this tiny **dissatisfaction** he was beginning to feel? He had a job and a position he enjoyed, a happy home, lovely kids who were doing well at school, yet he knew he was not **one hundred per cent satisfied** and involved as he had been several years before. Could it be **middle age**? At **forty-three**?

Chapter 3

Yetunde retired from the teaching profession. 'That's the first hurdle,' she told herself. 'If I don't have the courage to quit one job, I won't hunt seriously for another. First, I'll rest for a month or two.' This she did, and for a while she enjoyed being a full-time housewife and mother, but soon she got **bored** with it, and was gradually becoming **irritable** and frustrated because she could not get the type of job she wanted.

One day she had a phone call from Inyang.

'Yetunde? This is Inyang.'

'Hello, Inyang. It's nice to hear from you. How's the family?'

'Fine, thank you. I've been trying to get in touch with you all these weeks.'

'Is that so? I called the number you gave me several times, but it was always engaged.'

'That phone's been out of order for months. I'm calling from the shop. I came across your telephone number in one of my handbags only an hour ago.'

'Oh?'

'Look, someone told me you've retired from teaching.'

'Yes, I have at last.'

'What are you doing at the moment?'

'Nothing, just hanging around waiting for something suitable to turn up. I'm not in a hurry, but I must confess I'm getting bored with being a **full-time housewife**.'

'How would you like to come into **partnership** with me? My partner of some months has had to quit. She's just had a very rough deal from her husband so she needed the money to rebuild, and had to pull out.'

'Poor thing.'

'Yes, it's a shame. And after eighteen years of marriage too! The heartless man.

However, she'll recover. Do you like my proposal?'

'I like it. It sounds exciting, but give me a week to think it over, will you? I'll have to discuss it with my husband. How much will I have to contribute?'

'It'll be **twenty thousand naira** for a full partnership. Look, why don't you and your husband have dinner with John and me at our place in **Apapa** on Friday night? We could talk things over. I'm sure you'll have decided by then.'

'Okay, fine, Inyang. We'll do that. Thank you.'

'By the way, the dinner still stands even if your decision is "no".'

'All right. Thank you.'

After inspecting the shop and looking through the books with the help of an **accountant friend**, Chibuzor and his wife decided it was a good business venture and they put up the required capital. Glad of an opportunity to do something challenging,

Yetunde set about improving the art shop. At her suggestion, it was done up in **livelier colours** and **soft taped music** was introduced. They chose the name **Tundinyang Gift Centre** and instilled into their staff the importance of **good public relations**. Handouts were sent to reputable companies and they advertised regularly in the **news media**. Soon the shop began to attract a **superior clientele** and Inyang, who had criticised Yetunde's extravagance in the matter of the decor, had to agree that it had been money well spent. She was responsible for scouting around for good buys across the country, while Yetunde dealt with Lagos and the administrative side of the business. At first the profits flowed in but, as other gift shops began opening up around them, they found the competition **stiff** and had to work extra hard to stay on top.

Chibuzor was glad to see the **old sparkle** in his wife, although he now saw less of her due to her dedicated involvement in the running of the shop. He had been apprehensive at first that the children, who had of late been used to having their mother around all the time, would miss her, but discovered that they settled into the new routine without fuss. Yetunde, on the other hand, had been careful not to disrupt the family life too much. She did not leave everything in the hands of the nanny, but saw to breakfast and supper if she could, and she and her husband had lunch together once a week. On Saturdays, she worked only in the afternoons. What she earned went a long way towards easing the family's financial situation for, even after deduction by the bank for the loan they had taken, there was still something substantial for all those extras she had always longed for.

'Life's more fun now,' she told Chibuzor as they sat by a swimming pool in **Dakar, Senegal**, where they had taken the children for the **Easter holiday**.

'It's lovely here, but I miss my bed.' He hated sleeping in strange beds, no matter how plush they were.

'I know,' laughed his wife. 'You can't stop thinking about what type of people must have used the bedding.'

'Precisely. It makes my skin crawl.'

'Over here, Chi, old boy,' called **Segun Akanbi** one Sunday morning when Chibuzor entered the bar of his club after dropping Yetunde and the kids off at a nearby church.

'Boy, **Sege**! How are you and how's the family?' They shook hands.

'Fine, just fine. How's Yetunde?'

'She's all right.'

'Business doing fine? The shop's making lots of money?'

'Not lots, but business is good.'

'Great. It's becoming the "**in**" place for gifts, my wife told me.'

Chibuzor ordered a drink, and the two men were later joined by two other friends—**Jake** and **Abu**. They talked politics, business and, finally, women.

'Jake,' said Segun, 'Were you at **Tunji Ibrahim's** party at the **Frond Hall** last night? I couldn't go.'

'Boy!' said Jake. 'You surely missed something. What a party!'

'It was good?'

'Wow! You can say that again! Plenty of booze, plenty of food, and the place was crawling with **unattached dames** simply waiting for the kill. There were three **juju bands** each trying to outshout the other.'

'Well, he's got the money,' said Abu. 'He's a business tycoon, isn't he?'

'He is. Don't ask me what he buys or sells. You should have seen how money was "sprayed" on members of the bands who were singing his praise and that of his family, and also on the female dancers.'

'Oh yes? So the **spraying** was good, eh?'

'Too good. None of your **fifty-kobo** wads of

notes, thank you. It was the real stuff. **Twenty-naira notes**, all crisp and brand new. The women were well-prepared too. Many of them were armed with large handbags into which they stuffed the notes. I had to restrain myself from grabbing a handful of notes which floated carelessly to the ground, and making away with them.'

The others laughed. 'What was the man celebrating?' asked Chibuzor.

'The arrival of an **illegitimate son**,' replied Jake calmly.

'The what?'

'You heard. A son by one of his mistresses. That is, not born by his legally married wife with whom he lives.'

'What's so special about this son?'

'Nothing. Same anatomy as the rest of his species.'

'Perhaps he's the only son?'

'Nope. He's got three others, two at university.'

'He probably wanted an excuse to throw a party and spend a lot of money.'

'I don't think so. He can give a party any time he likes,' said Abu. 'He doesn't need an excuse. Anyway, the birth of a child is an occasion for joy.'

'That's true,' said Jake, 'but even if I had the money, you wouldn't catch me spending one-hundredth of what he spent on the christening of a child by my wife, let alone one by a mistress. There are better ways to which such money could be put. He could have had an orphanage built.'

'True. It was a foolish way of spending money.'

'Very foolish. Why, last year, when a girlfriend had twins for me, she wanted a party to celebrate. I told her to forget it and that if she insisted I would disown the children and she wouldn't see me for dust.'

'Jake,' said Chibuzor in surprise, 'do you really have children **out of wedlock**?'

'Yes, three. What's wrong with it?'

'Does **Bola** know?'

'Well, rumours got to her and she asked me about it but I denied it strongly.'

'You're a **coward**, Jake,' said Chibuzor. 'Why did you deny it?'

'No use upsetting the wife. I love her. She's one of the best women in the world, but she can make the home hell when roused. She'll get to know the truth one day. Then it will be less painful.'

'I don't agree,' said Segun. 'You're merely postponing the period of "hell". I have a daughter by a girlfriend and my wife knows about it. I told her myself. It was not a pleasant scene, but I assured her it was a mistake and that it would not happen again. She forgave me and even went round with presents for the baby later.'

'You too, Segun?' asked Chibuzor. 'What about you, Abu? Any confession to make too?'

'No, I'm glad to say. I don't believe in such things, for they cause complications later, and it is totally unnecessary when you have children already by your wife or wives.'

'Does it mean you have no girlfriends?' teased Jake.

'I do, from time to time, but I make it clear that I don't want babies from them. Apart from that, I never keep an affair going long enough for a woman to want to have a child with me. I love my wife and don't want to hurt her.'

'Me too,' said Segun. 'That girl was very stubborn. She deliberately allowed herself to get pregnant. It put me off her completely. My wife insists, however, that I give something towards the upkeep of the baby. Personally, I would prefer to forget both the mother and the baby.'

'You guys surprise me,' said Chibuzor. 'As middle-aged men, don't you feel a bit **reckless and irresponsible** carrying on the way you're doing? You ought to have finished **sowing your wild oats** by now and settled down to the serious task of bringing up your children and making plans towards a happy old age.'

The others roared with laughter.

'What's wrong with him? **Middle-aged** indeed! Life begins at forty!' said Jake, calling for another bottle of beer.

'Doesn't the man have a girlfriend?' asked Abu, amazed.

'No,' replied Chibuzor. 'I have not had an affair with anyone since I got married over sixteen years ago.'

'Is he joking? Is the man normal? Is he in good health?' Jake asked the world at large.

'It's true, Jake, as far as I know,' said Segun, laughing quietly. 'Chi has kept his marriage vows more than the rest of us. He's okay.'

'Not possible,' exclaimed Abu.

'Now come, Chi, are you serious about what you said?'

'Yes.'

'Then your behaviour is unusual. Something is wrong somewhere. It's people like you who tarnish the male image. You'd better see your doctor. **Low sex drive.**'

'Low sex drive nothing,' laughed Chibuzor. 'I'm perfectly normal. I don't have to be unfaithful to my wife to prove it.'

'Hear, hear,' said Segun. 'Ride on, Chi. Jake is a really bad boy. Give him a good talking to. He needs it or he'll father a whole village, like in that popular **Caribbean calypso.**'

'Maybe,' said Jake. 'Listen, Chi, you don't know what you're missing. Very shortly you'll be too old for all that and you'll regret not having made good use of this period of your life.'

'Well, we'll all get old some time. Seriously speaking, I think if a marriage has broken down, that's it. Re-marry if you like, or stay single and have fun. You might even decide to marry more than one wife, but to have affairs and kids here and there is irresponsible. Think of the future of these children and the effect on your homes.'

'Ah, well,' said Jake philosophically. 'We all

have to take a chance in life. Kids too. Besides, most men are really **polygamous at heart.**'

Chibuzor felt disgusted and changed the topic.

Some months later, he relived the above scene in his mind. Was there some truth in what the boys had said? Had he been missing something? Most of his friends had affairs and their marriages had stayed intact. Life with Yetunde was a lot of fun, and he would not like to hurt her, but **seventeen years** was a long time. It must be a record, judging by the way most marriages are these days. Would he look back later and wish he had behaved like his friends? Some naughty things he could chuckle over in his old age? No harm in trying. **Discretion** was the name of the game, and of course **one-night stands** only. No relationship to speak of, and so no silly ideas about having babies for him. To be fair to his conscience, he was not going out of his way to get anyone, but he was ready for **adventure**.

Yetunde walked briskly into the **Exhibition**

Hall of the **National Theatre**. She had never
heard of the artist whose work was being
exhibited, but Inyang had spoken glowingly
of him—one **Yinka Taiwo**. She sighed with
relief as she felt the coolness in the hall.
Sometimes the place was unbearably hot
and **claustrophobic**. There weren't many
people around. Someone handed her a
brochure and she wandered from painting
to painting. Many seemed **mediocre** to her,
but a few were particularly good. They
would sell well. She had been in the art shop
business for more than three years now and
she knew what her customers liked. She
lingered over one painting: that of the **sun
setting over the lagoon**. It was lovely, with
the pale blue water, the fishermen in their
canoes, and the **coconuts on the fringe of
the water**.

'I wonder how much this would cost.'

'Not much, madam,' said a voice behind her.

She was startled. She had not realised that
she had spoken aloud.

'Oh, excuse me,' she said as she stepped

back and bumped into a tall, thin man of about **thirty or so**.

'Steady, madam,' he said, picking up the leaflets she had dropped.

'Thank you.'

'That's all right, **Mrs Osaro**.'

'You know me?' she asked, surprised.

'I do indeed. A good student never forgets his teacher. You taught me several years ago at the **Technical College**.'

'Really?' She could not recall his face at all. 'What's your name?'

'Yinka Taiwo,' he said, smiling at her.

'Oh, you mean **this is your work**?'

'Yes, madam,' he said, bowing. *Hm! Pleasant man. Nice manners.*

'Lovely work, I must say,' she said.

'Thank you. I hope you'll patronise us. Our studio is at **Ikorodu Road**. Nothing elaborate. We live in a flat above the studio.

Ah, here comes my wife. **Sunbo**, darling, meet Mrs Osaro, the proprietress of **Tundinyang Art Shop**.'

'I'm very pleased to meet you, Mrs Osaro,' said Sunbo, a pretty lady of about **twenty-seven**. She was heavily pregnant. 'We were at the opening of your shop some years ago.'

'Were you? It was nice of you to come.'

'Yinka insisted we did. He said you were his favourite teacher at school. We never got round to congratulating you on that occasion because there were so many people, and you and your partner were constantly surrounded by well-wishers.'

'That was a pity. I'm always glad to meet my ex-students. I feel so proud. Is that your first child you're expecting?'

'No, the second. We have a son who's four,' said Yinka. 'Excuse me, please, Mrs Osaro. A friend is beckoning to me over there. If you're interested in this painting, please discuss the price with Sunbo. She takes care of that side of the business.' He bowed and left.

'Are you an artist too?' Yetunde asked
Sunbo.

'No, one is enough in the family. I did
banking and was working in a commercial
bank until eighteen months ago.'

'That's a good profession. It means money
from the business will be well taken care
of.'

'I hope so. That is, if we do make it. We're
just starting.'

Over the next few years, the business
relationship between Tundinyang and Yinka
Taiwo's studio grew steadily.

Oghogho, Yetunde's daughter, was now
seventeen and was awaiting her **G.C.E.
results**. She knew she would pass well, for
she had worked very hard. Her parents were
very proud of her and she was going to
follow in Daddy's footsteps and do
economics at university. She was a
pleasant, **gregarious** girl who had lots of
friends and was popular. She loved her
family. Chibuzor and Yetunde had always
been close to their children, who were

encouraged to bring their friends home, share whatever problems they had with their parents, and feel free to discuss any topic. As she grew older, Oghogho became appreciative of having such parents. Some of her friends hardly saw theirs, and those who did often could not discuss anything with them. At the age of twelve she had been told the **facts of life** and at sixteen allowed to date boys and bring them home. Oghogho felt proud that her parents trusted her. It made her feel grown-up and responsible. Recently, however, she had been feeling a bit low at not getting all the attention she used to get from them. **Dad always seemed to be at his Club**, and **Mum was totally absorbed in the art shop**. Why, she had not even noticed that **Bode**, Oghogho's current boyfriend, had not called for almost two weeks to take her out. Although there was the usual family conversation at breakfast and supper, did her parents really listen to what was said? They always seemed preoccupied. She had mentioned it to her brother **Efe** who was fifteen. No, he had not noticed any difference in their parents' behaviour.

Perhaps I'm oversensitive because of my tiff with Bode, thought Oghogho.

One Saturday afternoon, as she and Bode were driving home through a quiet street in **Surulere** after a party, she noticed a man and a woman, arms around each other, coming out of a **guest house**. They were walking towards a car. The man looked familiar. Oghogho turned to have a better look. **It was her father**. The woman was a stranger to her. At that moment the world stood still for her. Her father! The father she adored, condescending to do such a thing! What was happening? She sat bolt upright in her seat, her heart pounding, and stared straight ahead. Apparently, Bode had also seen the couple and had accelerated with the hope that Oghogho had not noticed anything. He was conversant with such incidents in life. He was **twenty-two** and a final-year student at the **University of Jos**. He came from a **broken home**, had had a succession of step-mothers, and was used to seeing his father with various mistresses. His mother had remarried. He liked the warmth in the Osaro family and envied the children for their relationship with their parents. How good it must be to have parents who actually listened to what you had to say, and who understood your various moods.

He glanced now at Oghogho and was alarmed at the way she sat still staring in front of her.

'Oghogho, Oghogho,' he said, raising his voice. He stopped the car. 'Oghogho,' he repeated, shaking her by the shoulder. She continued to stare. **He slapped her hard on the face.** She began to cry. He looked round. Luckily, it was a lonely road. He put his arm around her and rested her head on his shoulder and allowed her to cry. After some minutes he silently handed her his handkerchief. She dabbed at her eyes and blew her nose.

'Oghogho, darling,' he said gently after a while. 'Things like that happen, you know. It's part of adult life.' He had seen Mr Osaro with women on several occasions in that part of Lagos and at first had felt a bit disappointed, but he had not lost any respect for the man. After all, he was being very discreet about it, and there might be a good reason for his behaviour. He probably had problems with his wife. **You never really knew.** From the little experience he had had, he knew that some women were cold and that physical appearance had nothing to do with **sexual prowess**.

'Please take me to the shop,' said Oghogho, after she had calmed down. 'I would like to see my mother.'

'What for? Shouldn't I take you home or, better still, take you for a drive while you collect yourself?'

'No, thank you, Bode. I want to see her. I'm okay now. Let's go, she might still be there.'

Mrs Osaro and Inyang were preparing to shut for the evening when they arrived there.

'Hello, Mum. Hello Auntie,' said Oghogho, pretending to be as happy and carefree as usual.

'Hello, Oghogho, how are you?' asked

Inyang.

'Fine, thank you, Auntie.'

'Yetunde, aren't you lucky? Here's another member of your family coming to see you even though it's almost time for you to go home.'

'Yes, I'm lucky. Oghogho, your Dad has just called here on the way back from his Club.'

'Dad has been here?' asked Oghogho sharply, looking at her mother in surprise.

'Yes, why? He normally does on Saturdays. You look surprised.'

'No, nothing.'

'Look, Yetunde,' said Inyang, 'I must go now. We have a dinner engagement. See you on Monday.'

'Goodnight, Inyang. Have a lovely weekend. I'm leaving soon, too.'

'Now, young lady,' Yetunde said to her daughter as soon as Inyang had left, 'Tell Mummy all. Why have you been crying?'

'Me? Crying?' attempted Oghogho, light-heartedly.

'Oh, come on,' said her mother impatiently. 'What's the matter?'

Oghogho looked at her searchingly. She looked tired but happy and was very attractive in her lace **buba and wrapper**. Her lipstick was a little bit smudged. *From kissing Daddy, no doubt! Poor thing! If only you knew!* thought Oghogho. She felt like putting a protective arm around her. How could her father behave like that? Things would never be the same again. She did not really know why she had wanted to see her mother so urgently. She couldn't possibly tell her about her father. Her mother would be terribly hurt and might decide to leave home without demanding an explanation. She had so much trust in her husband. Oghogho couldn't bear her home being broken up like some of her friends'—Ngozi, Tessy, Femi, the list was endless. Oh, no! Hadn't she read somewhere that **what you did not know would not hurt you**?

'Nothing, Mum. Bode and I went to a party

and...'

'Oh, Bode's here?' said her mother with relief and a smile. *Perhaps they had quarrelled,* she thought. 'Ask him to come and say hello to me. I like that boy.'

'There's no need to ask him in, Mum, you said you were leaving for home soon. Besides, we're going to the pictures. I just called to tell you.'

'All right, darling. Have a nice time. See you later.'

Business was slack one afternoon and Yetunde was alone in the office doodling on a pad when there was a knock on the door and **Yinka Taiwo** strolled in.

'Good evening, madam,' he greeted, flashing his even white teeth.

Yetunde looked up. 'Come in, Yinka. It's been a long time. How's the family? No need to ask, actually. Sunbo was here this morning to collect a check. Have you something for us?' She was always pleased to see him on the rare occasions he decided to call at the shop. Usually business was done through Sunbo.

'Everyone is fine, madam. I came to see a friend nearby and I thought I should look in and say "hi" to you and Mrs Akpan.'

'That's nice of you. Won't you sit down? Mrs Akpan's just left for home. She had a headache. How's business? The work Sunbo brought in last week was simply marvellous. The things were **snapped up** within a few days.'

'Good. I'm delighted.' He shut the door and leaned against it. He looked at her with a faraway look in his eyes. Yetunde became a bit nervous.

'Won't you sit down?' she repeated. 'You're behaving strangely.'

'Am I?' he asked absentmindedly. Suddenly, he strode towards her, grabbed her and kissed her fiercely on the lips. He released her just as quickly.

She sat back weakly in her chair. Quick as it had been, she had been **excited by the kiss**, but now she wished she had pushed him away at that moment. But how was she to know what was coming? Things had happened too fast for her. She sat up straight and hoped she looked quite stern.

'Now, may I know the meaning of that?'

'Yetunde, I'm in love with you.'

'In love with me! You can't be serious. When did this **illness** of yours begin?'

'Don't talk about my affection for you in that flippant fashion. I've tried for ages to curb my feelings but I can't any longer. I have always loved you right from the Technical School. I have lots of admiration for you and I dream always of taking you into my arms and telling you how much I love you.' He moved towards her again. This time she was prepared. She pushed him away, and got up.

'Yinka, what exactly do you think you're playing at? This is not a nursery school, you know. I'm a **respectably married woman** and quite happy with my husband. I'm prepared to forgive what has taken place this afternoon, but it must not be repeated.'

'It's only the beginning, Yetunde,' he said softly. 'I love you. What have you got against me?'

'Heavens!' she cried exasperatedly. 'Have I not just explained things to you? I'm happily married and I don't need an affair. Perhaps you're too young to take that in.'

'Young?' he laughed. 'I'm thirty-six, you know. You're not that much older than I am, so please don't talk to me as if I were a **wayward child**.'

'However, age is beside the point. I don't want to see you here again. We shall continue to do business with your wife, but if you insist on calling on me then we shall stop business with your studio altogether.'

He gave a short laugh. If only she knew how hard it had been trying to persuade Sunbo that they should keep on supplying Tundinyang, whose orders were the lowest and the cheapest among their numerous customers. He had become well-known and his work was very much in demand. He knew Yetunde's taste and always kept back some special pieces to be sold to her at moderate prices. She did not know about this, and he was not going to tell her that his wife thought it was a waste of time doing business with her shop. He was very much in love with her and would at all costs like to maintain the only link between them, even though it annoyed Sunbo.

After he had left, Yetunde sat thinking **nice thoughts**. She was **flattered** that a younger man found her attractive and had admired her for so long. She had been surprised rather than annoyed by his behaviour, but she was not going to encourage him. She had always found him nice and pleasant and liked him, although she had never entertained any romantic notions about him. In fact, she had been so absorbed in her family and in her jobs over the years that she had not flirted with any man, even in thought or by look. She went to the full-length mirror in the corner of the room and took a critical look at herself. Not bad for her age. She still cut quite a **youthful figure** and looked years younger than Yinka. His kiss lingered on her lips. She felt **guilty**. *I've cheated on Chi,* she thought.

When later she told Inyang about the incident, the latter confessed that Yinka had confided in her many months before that he was in love with Yetunde and was going to tell her about it. She had warned him to keep off, as Yetunde had eyes only for her husband.

'But he can't be in love with me,' said Yetunde, perplexed. 'He loves his wife and children. At least I deduced that from the way he talks about them and looks after them. What does he want with his **ex-teacher**?'

'You've always been a very attractive person, Yetunde, so you should expect this sort of thing. He's nice too.'

'I like him, but having an affair is out of the question for me. Chibuzor and I have never been unfaithful to each other. There's absolutely no reason to be.'

Inyang gave her a brief amused look, and thought of the night out she had had with

Chibuzor in Onitsha the previous year when they had met accidentally in a hotel at which they had both been staying. He was there for a conference and she had gone to see her daughter who was in a boarding school. She had always admired his **burly looks** and she had not wanted to miss the opportunity of getting closer to him. She had asked him to take her to the pictures. He could not refuse as they were family friends. Afterwards she had invited him to her room for drinks, **one thing led to another** and he ended up spending the night there. The next day he could not get away from her fast enough and since then had avoided her as much as he decently could without arousing suspicion. She had been elated at the time because as well as finding Chibuzor attractive, it was also a way of **getting her own back at Yetunde** for the way she and her friends despised her all those years ago in their class in Zaria when they treated her like an **outcast**.

Yinka did not give up trying to woo Yetunde. He kept ringing her up to tell her how much he loved her, and trying to persuade her to let him see her. When she would no longer take his calls, he began to send her **love notes and poems**. She was secretly thrilled and found it all very **romantic**, but she refused to yield. As time went on, thoughts of him began to creep in at disturbing moments like when she was in her husband's arms or had watched a romantic film. She knew she was becoming more and more fond of him. Perhaps if they had both been uncommitted something deeper might have sprung up. As things were, she had a perfect marriage and she did not want an affair.

One day, **Ronke Otabor**, a long-time but casual friend of hers, rang her up to invite her for drinks at her house in Surulere.

'What are you celebrating?' teased Yetunde. 'Do you and **Fred** feel guilty about not sharing all that wealth around enough?'

'Nothing of the kind,' said Ronke. 'I just thought that a few of us who used to work for **Owens International** should get together, put our feet up, and discuss old times.'

'Good idea, but I don't know if I can make it. Business, you know...'

'Oh, you must come, Yetunde,' said Ronke urgently. 'Let Inyang work hard for a change instead of having a nice time running all over the country saying she's looking for bargains. The lazy thing! Everyone knows that you do all the hard work there. You look out or she'll **pull a fast one** on you.'

'Easy does it now, Ronke. I can see that you've not forgiven Inyang for buying that plot of land you and Fred had set your mind on.'

'Well, would you? After all, I only told her about it because we were close friends. I asked her if it was good for the price and she sneaked off, made a better offer, and bought it. I'll get even with her some time. However, Yetunde, you must come to this little gathering. I'll send my driver for you.'

'I'll try to come. Maybe it would do me some good to get away from the shop for a couple of hours. I'll find my way. It's the same address, isn't it?'

'It is, but my driver will come for you,' insisted Ronke. 'You should relax more. Try to be ready by **four o'clock**.'

Yetunde was surprised to find no other guest at Ronke's that Saturday when she got there. She asked if she was too early, and it was then that her friend confessed that there was actually **no party taking place** and she had wanted Yetunde to be at her place that day.

'There's no party?' asked Yetunde, bewildered. 'You just wanted me to come here? Why?' She wondered if her friend had gone mad.

'Listen, Yetunde. I have my reasons for asking you to come. **Seeing is believing**. I don't know if I've made the right decision or not, but at least I have eased my conscience.'

'What's the matter, Ronke?' asked Yetunde, more mystified than ever.

'Briefly, it's this. Come over to this window.

You see that **guest house** two houses away?'

'Yes. The one on your side of the road.'

'Yes. You see, your husband has been bringing women there for the past **two years**. At least that was when I first noticed. Usually, it's a different one every other Saturday. I just stumbled on this by chance. I was cooking in my kitchen when I looked up and saw him sitting out with a woman on the balcony at the back of the guest house. They were having a drink. Afterwards, they went in. You have a better view of the balcony from my kitchen, but your husband always parks his car on the other side of the street, so we'll see him from here if he turns up today. Occasionally, he doesn't.'

Long before Ronke finished her explanation, Yetunde had collapsed into the nearest chair. **Chibuzor!** Chibuzor, with another woman? Unthinkable! She felt faint. Ronke poured out some **brandy** for both of them.

'But what would my husband want with another woman when our marriage is so good?' she asked as soon as she felt a little bit stronger.

'Oh well, you know what men are. **Variety** and all that stuff.'

'Why didn't you tell me sooner? I know we don't see each other often, but something as serious as this threatens a friend's home...'

'I didn't want to alarm you unnecessarily. It is difficult telling anyone that their partner is having an affair. You feel guilty if the marriage later **hits the rocks**. However, as I told you before, your husband usually brought a different woman each time. To me, that meant that he was just having a **lark**—nothing serious. The fact that he took the trouble to bring them to an **out-of-the-way area** like ours confirmed what I thought. I didn't think there was any threat to your marriage. But he's been coming with the **same woman** now for the past **four months**, so I thought it might be getting serious. Deciding to tell you about it was not easy, I can assure you.'

'What does she look like, this woman?'

'You'll soon find out. What time is it? **Four**

thirty-five? They'll be here shortly if they are coming today.'

'If they don't, I'm prepared to keep coming here every Saturday until they do.'

'Ah, here they come,' whispered Ronke. 'I must say your husband likes to be **punctual**.'

Yetunde went to the window on **trembling legs**. Sure enough, there was the familiar figure of Chibuzor. He had got out of the car and was helping the lady out. They walked **hand-in-hand** towards the guest house. Her heart began to race. She felt dizzy and Ronke put an arm around her and led her back to her chair. She poured herself some more brandy and began to drink it slowly.

'I almost wish I hadn't asked you to come,' began Ronke dejectedly. 'You see, something like this happened to Fred and me once. He was carrying on a hectic love affair with this pretty **divorcee** in his office. I knew her quite well. We met regularly at official functions and were on nodding terms, but I didn't suspect a thing. How could I? Fred and I were very fond of each other and everything was super. It still is, I'm glad to say.'

'Lucky thing.'

'I guess so. Well, out of the blue, another colleague of my husband's, a lady, came and told me what was going on. I couldn't believe my ears. The affair had been going on for over a year; she decided to tell me because the woman and Fred had been **house-hunting**! He was going to leave me and the children! I went wild!'

'I would too.'

'I fought with Fred, tore up every shirt he had, and damaged half the things we owned. I really went to extremes! The children thought I had gone mad. Later, I calmed down and we talked things over. Do you know that Fred was actually glad that I knew of the relationship? It made it easier for him to break with the woman whom he had begun to find a **bore**. Men are such cowards!'

'Did the woman give up that easily?'

'No, but Fred had made up his mind that he
was having nothing more to do with her.
She finally left the company in anger.'

'He couldn't have seriously been involved
with her.'

'Maybe not. Many good marriages could be
saved if couples maintained the interest
they have in each other as they get older.
We sort of **took each other for granted**.
Fred later told me that if I had cared enough
I ought to have noticed a change in him and
the affair would not have gotten as far as it
had.'

Yetunde sat in silence for a few minutes,
then suddenly burst out laughing. Ronke
looked at her with concern.

'Are you all right?'

'I'm all right. I'm really very grateful to you
for taking the **bold step** of bringing this to
my notice. Not many people would have the
courage. I wouldn't. What amuses me is that
the lady is neither young nor pretty. In fact,
she's **fat and ugly**.'

'Well, she's plump and must be about **thirty-eight or so**.'

'And here I am killing myself with a strict diet so as to stay slim and pretty for Chibuzor while he amuses himself with **fat women**. When he leaves here on Saturdays he usually looks in at the shop to say he is just on his way back from his club. How could I have been so blind? I never suspected a thing. He would kiss me affectionately, and I never smelt any strange perfume.'

'Naturally not. You were not expecting to.'

Suddenly Yetunde became angry. She jumped up. 'Here, Ronke, give me a **knife**.'

'A knife!' cried the other, alarmed. 'What for?'

'To **slash the tyres** of Chibuzor's car.'

'Oh, what good would that be?'

'At least, he won't be able to take that **tart** home in our car. He'll have to put her in a taxi. I feel like doing something to hurt him right now. Or would you advise my going over to the guest house to join them? That might be a better idea.'

'Oh, no,' said Ronke hastily. 'That wouldn't do at all. Still, to me, slashing tyres is a bit expensive. Learn from my experience. Fred and I spent two years trying to replace the things I had smashed, and there were some that can never be replaced. I regretted my action later. I could have handled the matter in a less expensive way and achieved the same result.'

'But I feel like doing something now. Something that would **shake Chibuzor** before he comes home to a real live battle. I know. I'll **deflate his tyres**.' She got up, took her handbag, and rushed out of the house, followed by Ronke who was getting excited and did not want to miss a thing.

Chibuzor's blood froze when a boy ran upstairs to tell him that a lady was deflating his tyres. He went to the window and watched as his wife set about it in a determined manner. He sat down heavily in a chair, put his head in his hands, and

groaned. What was this? Would Yetunde leave him? He couldn't bear that. He loved her dearly. What explanation could he give for his behaviour? Oh dear! Would the children know? That would be terrible! **Oghogho** in particular must never know. She was very sensitive. What was he to do? Get friends to intercede with Yetunde? No, it was something for the two of them only. Oh dear!

He looked at his companion malevolently. She stared back unconcernedly. She was glad that Chibuzor's wife had discovered their affair. Now she would know exactly where she stood with him—whether he would leave his wife for her or not. It would be nice to have a man around the house once more. She was glad that she had not agreed to his nonsense of not wanting to see her any more. **Weeping and clinging to him** had done the trick and he had continued seeing her. What woman would see such a **good catch** and throw away her chance? She was prepared to be his second or third wife. That was the **"in"** thing in the country these days, after all.

Chibuzor got up and gave her a **twenty naira note**. 'Here, **Ayi**, take a taxi home. I'm sorry I can't give you a lift back.'

'I'll wait until you fix the tyres. I'm not in a hurry. The children are all right with the nanny.'

'I don't care,' said Chibuzor, irritated. Was the woman so dense? One would expect her to offer to quit the scene. 'Please go.'

'When do we see?'

'We don't. Just go away.'

'But I'm not responsible for what has happened.'

'I didn't say you were. Now, please go, will you? I need to think.'

'Chibuzor, you know how much I love you; you can't leave me just because that woman has found out about us. What has she got that I don't have? Just because you met her first...'

'Shut up, Ayi, and stop acting. You have other male friends, besides I told you several weeks ago that our relationship must come to an end.'

'Yes, but it hasn't. You love me and...'

'I'll have to leave you here then, Ayi, since you're being so unco-operative.'

She got up, collected her things, and grudgingly left the room, hoping that he would contact her later.

He went to the window again. How had Yetunde got to know? The lady with her looked familiar. She probably lived in the area. How foolish he had been. He should not have stuck to a particular guest house. He was too conservative. Well, he'd have to figure out how best to approach his wife.

She was waiting for him when he got home. She had taken their younger boys to her parents' for the weekend. Oghogho and Efe were away at school, and **Udoh** had gone to his room.

She rushed at him and held him by his shirt as soon as he stepped into the house, and for the next three minutes she shouted herself hoarse saying whatever came into her head. When she ran out of words, he led her to a settee and sat down with her, cradling her in his arms. She began to cry. This disarmed him and he did not know where to begin his explanation.

'I'm sorry, darling,' he attempted, 'to have caused you so much distress. I can neither explain my action nor justify it, but please believe me when I say that **these affairs meant nothing to me**.'

'If they meant nothing to you, why did you keep on having them? It's been going on for years, hasn't it?'

'Let's not go into all the details, Yetunde. It isn't necessary. Listen, I love you and you're the only woman for me. There's never been any doubt about that. Our marriage was never threatened.'

'But this last one was getting serious, wasn't it?'

'No, it wasn't. Far from it. She's a **widow** with three children. She's rather lonesome and I...'

'How kind of you, **Sir Galahad**! So you felt it was incumbent on you to keep her company and make her happy,' said Yetunde bitterly.

'No, my love, calm down. Look, I'm extremely sorry for what has taken place, but let me point out that I'm not unique in succumbing to temptations of this sort. Try to understand and forgive me. We have a very good marriage and I have no reason to be unfaithful to you. Still, these things happen. It's all part of living.'

'Will it not happen again?'

'It would be easy to say it won't, but let's be realistic, nothing is certain in life.'

'Have you no self-control over such things? I have not looked at any other man since we met. It does not appeal to me. If you really love me, you wouldn't want to make love to any other woman, don't you feel that way?'

'Sure I do,' he said. It would be hard to convince her that to a man, a physical relationship with a woman does not always involve the heart. He was truly ashamed of himself and sorry for all he had done, but he

could not promise that it would never occur
again. He ardently wished he could, but that
would be hypocritical. He would try his best
not to hurt his wife, although he had
enjoyed these flings, he could not imagine
life without her. She had brought him so
much joy.

Although she forgave him, Yetunde felt
shocked and empty. To the best of her
ability she had tried to be a good wife,
mother, lover, and friend to her family. The
discovery that her husband had been having
affairs had shaken her more than she would
care to admit to herself or let be known. The
whole thing made her feel **inadequate**—she,
who had always been so sure of herself. She
felt she had not played her role successfully.
Were the children dissatisfied with her too,
and were they finding solace somewhere
else or in something else? You never can tell
until something **blows up in your face** and
you have to halt in your tracks to reflect.
How could she and her husband have been
so close to each other and yet he could still
deceive her for so long? She felt fury in her

heart. It would be a long time before she
ever trusted anyone again.

Chapter 4

Yetunde was very surprised when she got home one evening to find **Yinka Taiwo** having a drink in the garden with **Chibuzor**. She had not seen him for months nor heard from him, and had concluded that he had got over his infatuation for her. He looked very relaxed and attractive. She was full of suppressed excitement as they shook hands. *"I'm not as indifferent to him as I thought,"* she told herself. He looked straight into her eyes, but she averted them and turned to her husband who gave her a kiss and asked Udoh to get her a drink.

'Yinka was calling on some friends around here and he decided to come in and say "hi" to us,' said Chibuzor after pulling out a chair for her.

'Very nice of you, Yinka,' she murmured. 'How's the family?'

'Fine, Mrs Osaro. I saw your partner the other day and she told me business was so good you're thinking of using the empty shop next to you as a **restaurant**.'

'I don't know about business being so good, but we're indeed thinking of opening a restaurant.'

'How soon?'

We don't know, as we've not been given the shop yet. The management of the Square hasn't quite made up its mind whether it would like a restaurant in that building or not. We've only made the proposal to them.'

'Oh, it's like that, is it? Actually, I told Mrs Akpan I would be interested in doing up the place—my boys are quite good—and she said I should have a chat with you about it.'

'All right, when we're ready, we'll give you first consideration if your charges are right and we can afford it.'

'Money is no problem with Tundinyang. We know that. None of your cheques to us has ever bounced.'

'Don't be too sure,' she said lightly. 'Competition in the gift shop line is becoming keen these days and we have to keep on our toes all the time. Chi, has **Oghogho** arrived for the weekend yet? I was going to pick her up at the campus, but she rang to say **Bode** would. I hope he was able to leave the office early enough to do so.'

'They came back ages ago, but went out almost at once. They had something lined up for the evening. She promised to be home early and said to tell you not to fret.'

'I won't. She should have waited to say "hello" before dashing out again. Ah well...' The telephone rang.

'I'll get it,' said Chibuzor, getting up.

'Why did you come, Yinka?' asked Yetunde as soon as they were alone.

He raised his eyebrows innocently. 'I was just passing by and I...'

'Oh, come on. I'm quite sure you don't have friends you call on around here, and you could have asked **Sunbo** to discuss the restaurant thing with me.'

'I guess I could have, but I wanted to see you, Yetunde. I love you. Why do you keep refusing to see me? You're treating me as if I'm a kid who doesn't know what he's about. I'm a man and I love and want you.'

'That's nicely put, Yinka, but as I've said before, please don't call to see me here or anywhere else. You'll only cause trouble. Are you out to upset my home? If you're really fond of me, you would respect my wishes.'

'I would, but not in this case. You're being unfair to me. When a man declares his love for a lady, she could at least give him a chance to get close to her. If she finds him unpleasant, she could send him away. But you're being difficult. You won't even try to get to know me. You keep pushing me away as if I have a **contagious disease**.'

'Well, you do, don't you?' she laughed, amused at his outburst.

'Don't you care for me at all?'

'That's not the point.' She realised she had said the wrong thing as this would probably encourage him. 'Er, what I mean is no, I don't.'

'I'm not convinced.'

At that moment her husband came back. 'Guess what, Yetunde,' he said, picking her up and whirling her around.

'Set me down, Chi. I feel dizzy.' She tried to regain her breath. 'What's happened? Have we hit the **jackpot**?'

'That was my mother. **Ivie** has had her baby—a boy.'

'Hurrah,' she cried, jumping up and hugging him. 'After **five girls**. That's great! **Sola** will be so thrilled.'

'This calls for a celebration.'

'Yes, and wc must leave for **Ogba** tomorrow morning. I must go and lend a hand for the weekend or possibly longer if I can. Mama won't be able to cope now that the older girls are all away.'

'That's kind of you, darling,' he said, touched. He took her in his arms and kissed her passionately. They forgot all about Yinka, who coughed discreetly and quietly took his leave.

Outside, he sat in his car for a while before driving off. He felt **jealous**. How could he make Yetunde see that he really loved her and had always done so? He had even courted and married his wife partly because she looked slightly like her. What did she see in that **bear-like** husband of hers who must be incredibly dull?

He was convinced that he was more capable of taking care of her in terms of love and comfort. How he would cherish her! He thought of his wife and their children. He loved them but he wanted to spend the rest of his life with Yetunde. Did she care? He would have to find out. Something told him that she did not find him repulsive—that look of delight on her face each time they met must mean something.

Yetunde spent a very busy fortnight in Ogba looking after her sister-in-law and her

children, and came back to Lagos exhausted
and with several problems. Her daughter,
who was preparing for her examinations,
had overworked herself and fallen ill and
had had to be admitted into the health
centre at the campus. Her second son had
been **suspended** from his school for
smoking cigarettes on the school premises.
Business in the art shop had **ground almost
to a halt**; two of the three shop assistants
had resigned after being accused of theft by
Inyang, who, instead of replacing the staff,
had taken off on a **cruise** with her family.
With no supervision, the girl left there could
not cope—opening when she liked and
leaving the place unattended—so Yetunde
spent her first week back hurriedly
recruiting staff and making daily visits to
Oghogho. It was hectic and she felt **used**.
Why should all this happen when she had
been helping other people with their
problems? Things ought to have gone
smoothly for her. She felt angry at the way
Inyang, while enjoying a large share of the
profits from the shop, left most of the
headaches to her. She felt cheated and
thought of pulling out of the business, but

had to shelve the idea when she thought of all that would be involved—looking for a suitable place, finding adequate capital, establishing new clientele, etc. She didn't feel she had the energy yet.

She was angry too at the way Chibuzor took things calmly. When she accused him of being indifferent to family problems, he said he was watching his **blood pressure** and that there was no need to get unduly worked up. Oghogho was getting better and was shortly to be discharged; **Uyi** was only going through a phase—smoking cigarettes did not mean that he had joined a bad gang; other assistants would be recruited for the shop and business would pick up. She wished she could see the situation that way but she couldn't. The pressure was too great for her and she felt like getting away from it all. They could not afford a **holiday abroad** that year because of the heavy **mortgage** on their house. How lucky Inyang was to be able to take off with her family at any time. Money wasn't their problem. She began to long for those **carefree pre-marriage days** when only the best of everything would do and the sense of responsibility was less.

She was locking up her car at the car park one afternoon when someone hailed her from behind. She did not need to turn to know that it was Yinka Taiwo.

'Good evening, Yetunde,' he greeted her with a **boyish smile**.

'Oh, hello, Yinka,' she said, her eyes lighting up, for as usual she was pleased to see him. 'Shopping around here?'

'Yes. I came to get a card and a present for Sunbo. It's our **wedding anniversary** tomorrow.'

'That's great. Congratulations! I hope you got her something nice.'

'I think so. It's something she's always wanted. Look, Yetunde, can I talk to you for a few minutes? Or can you tell me when I can come and see you? You cannot continue refusing to see me. It's unfair. You should at least give yourself a chance to know me.

What are you afraid of? That you will fall in love with me?'

'Oh, come off it, Yinka, don't be ridiculous. We're both adults and married to other people. Let's behave sensibly.'

'Precisely what I thought to myself.'

'What did you think?'

'That we should go somewhere quiet and talk things over. I won't take "no" for an answer,' he added as she began to protest. She found herself being led to his car. Neither of them said a word as they drove through the quiet and cool evening to the **beach**. Night was falling fast and the place was almost empty. They got out of the car and walked on the cool fine sand towards the sea. She took off her shoes, very conscious of his nearness.

She at first resisted when he took her in his arms but, as he would not let her go and began to kiss her, she relaxed and responded to his kisses. When he released her she turned away from him feeling very confused. *Why am I here? Why did I allow him to kiss me? What will this lead to? I should be ashamed of myself.* But she wasn't—instead she began to feel an **inward glow**.

He was a bit taken aback by her sudden reaction. From her kisses he had been quite sure a few minutes back that she was not totally indifferent to him. And now? Was it remorse at having let herself go for a second?

He approached her hesitantly. 'Yetunde, are you angry with me? Perhaps I should have asked you first but I couldn't help myself. I just had to kiss you.'

'Who told you I'm angry?' she asked, turning back, smiling.

'My mistake then, sweetheart,' he said, opening his arms to her.

She suddenly felt young and light-hearted. 'You'll have to catch me first,' she said as she broke into a run, stumbling over the sand.

'Very well,' he said, gathering up his **agbada** and running after her.

A group of fishermen bringing in the evening's catch gaped at them in surprise as they raced past, panting from the exercise.

'Abi de woman don go crazy and de man wan catch am,' said one to his colleagues.

'Ah, make we help am. Dem be like rich people and he fit gif us money.'

'Oga, make we help you catch am?' another called after Yinka.

'No, thank you,' he called back. *'I go catch am myself.'*

The fisherman shrugged and went back to his friends. *'Maybe two of dem dey craze,'* he declared.

When Yetunde got to the car, Yinka was nowhere in sight. She felt very hot and began to mop her brow. Some minutes later he walked up thoughtfully, carrying two large paper bags full of **shells**.

'What are you going to do with all those?' she asked curiously.

'You'll see. An idea just occurred to me as I passed by the stall where they were being sold. I want to make something that will always remind both of us of this, our **first meeting**.'

'Is this our first meeting?'

'First date, yes. In the sense of **boy meets girl**. So, it has to be marked somehow.'

She was touched and impressed. Here was someone even more **romantic and dreamy** than herself. 'I lost the race,' he said as he started the car. 'I'll have to think of another way to earn my kiss.'

When she got home that evening, she expected her husband to notice a difference in her, for she certainly felt different, but he did not. He greeted her as warmly as usual and they had a brief talk about the sort of day they had had, then he retired behind the papers as he had begun to do lately.

Dinner was a quiet affair now that all the children were away at boarding schools. This had been a period of her life that she had looked forward to, when she and her husband would be alone without all the bustle and they could take off anywhere at any time without feeling that the children were being neglected. But things had not worked out quite that way. Chibuzor hated travelling and being away from all the comforts and the familiar atmosphere of his home. He said he felt too old to be dragged all over the place. He had even begun to find going to parties an **ordeal** and they limited themselves to official ones and they did not entertain as much as they used to. He spent most of his spare time reading, gardening, or at his club. She loved these things too but thought they were too young to have such set ways. 'What will we do when we're old and grey?' she asked him several times. 'At this rate, we'll be **senile** in no time for, after all, you're only **fifty** and I'm still a long way from it.' He laughed and said that he would be a lot more active when he retired from service, for at the moment work sapped all his energy. 'By the time he retires we'll be too old to enjoy travelling,' she told herself. She could not really complain because he was good to her and the children and that was important. They were still quite close even though she could not bring herself to be as loving towards him as she was before discovering his affairs with other women. They rarely referred to the subject and when they did they had a laugh over it, or at least she pretended to. A friend had told her that was the best way to bear it. 'Take it lightly provided he showed regrets.' Well, she had, and was still very fond of him. If only life could be more exciting with him!

After their first date, Yetunde and Yinka began to see each other **once a week**. They both looked forward to it and usually met at her insistence in **out-of-the-way places**. When he asked her if she was ashamed to be seen with him, she told him that, apart from the fact that they were both married, it would not do for her, the wife of a **high public officer**, to be seen with another man in public places. Tongues were bound to start wagging, and she did not want a **scandal**. They had to think of their respective partners and their families. He did not agree with her. If she liked his company as she had said, then they should be able to meet anywhere without giving a damn about what others thought. For his part, he was in love with her, and, if given the chance, would like all and sundry to know about it. She did not take him seriously. They were both out for a bit of fun for a short while and that would be that.

She was puzzled, however, when after several months he did not demand any **physical relationship** with her. Was that not what an affair was supposed to be all about? It was not for lack of privacy, for he had taken an apartment in a secluded part of **Ebute Metta**, which they both took pleasure in decorating to their taste. "**Our place**," they called it. There they talked, drew sketches, painted, or sometimes sat companionably watching the television or video films. Occasionally they went out for a meal or drinks.

One day he gave her a beautifully wrapped parcel. Inside, was a glass-framed velvet board on which tiny brightly painted shells had been carefully arranged. To the ordinary eye it depicted the merging of two trees with a heart at the common stem. She knew it was something else.

'It's **two Ys**,' she told him when he asked her to guess what it symbolised.

'Clever girl. It's **Yetunde and Yinka** forever in love,' he said softly as they stood admiring it after hanging it up on the wall.

'It's beautiful, Yinka. Simply exquisite. You're so gifted.'

'I'm glad you like it. It's a souvenir of our first date. **We belong together.**'

She looked at him with some concern. Was their relationship going to get out of hand? Could she handle it? Although she would not own up to it, she knew she was gradually **falling in love with him**. She decided to nip things in the bud by not showing up the next week for their usual **Thursday date**. He rang her at work the next day to find out what happened. He had spent a sleepless night thinking about her. So had she. They agreed to meet that evening since it was obvious they could not wait till the following Thursday to see each other.

He pulled her into his arms as soon as she entered the flat.

'Don't ever do that again, Yetunde. You gave me a fright when you failed to turn up yesterday.'

'Why?'

'I thought something had happened to you. You mean a lot to me. If you had decided not to come, you should have rang me up.'

'I'm sorry, Yinka. You see, I was confused.'

'What's the matter? Don't you like me at all? You've never said you love me, but I'm prepared to wait. You'll come round to it one of these days. Are you really indifferent to me?'

'I'm not, but I'm frightened about the way you feel about me—the intensity. You're taking the whole thing too seriously.'

'I'm seriously in love with you.'

'You can't be. It isn't right. We have partners and...'

'Well, there you have the position in a nutshell. What are you going to do about it?'

They made love for the first time that day and she went away feeling more confused because she realised that this was no light-hearted affair that they could easily put an end to whenever they wished. What had she let herself in for now? She would have liked to be with him every minute of the day if she could, and she knew he felt the same. She was deliriously happy, but the necessity for **secrecy** about the relationship and the longing to be with him, it was so strenuous for her that she began to lose weight. He laughed when she told him her fears.

'You're wasting your time,' he told her. 'My prayers will be answered and **everything will come out into the open.**'

'Why?'

'I want everyone to know how I feel about you. I hate **clandestine activities**. I love you and want us to be together.'

'How?' she asked, surprised. 'What about our families? We cannot abandon them.'

'True. I'll make provision for mine. I'm fond of Sunbo and the children and I'll keep them in comfort as much as I can, but I would like to spend the rest of my life with you.'

'It's easy for a man. I'm a mother and the thought of abandoning my children fills me with guilt, much as I would like to stay close to you.'

'That's the closest you've come to saying you love me,' he teased. 'You're so **reserved and cautious**.'

'Can't we continue like this? Still be with our respective partners?'

'Would you want that? I wouldn't. What I would like is a more domestic atmosphere—in short, to live like husband and wife in the real sense.'

She could not help laughing. 'Grow up, Yinka. You've forgotten how old I am. I may not be able to give you children and I'm not anxious to mess around again with **nappies** after all these years.'

'Who talked about children? I already have four and Sunbo and I have decided that that's all we'll have.'

'If we set up home together, you might want one from me and I may be too old then.'

'Relax, Yetunde, and stop putting obstacles in the way.'

She looked at him curiously. His attitude was strange. He was not after sex, he did not want children from her, but he wanted them to desert their respective partners and get married. The situation was **ridiculous** to say the least. He must be play-acting, trying to realise the dreams he had while at the Technical School. Shortly he would wake up, get fed up with their little game and they would stop seeing each other. She should be prepared for that, but she had become so involved with him that such a thought was unbearable. Where did Chibuzor stand? She could not possibly leave him.

One afternoon **Sunbo** called at the shop to see Yetunde. She looked very miserable.

'Hello, Sunbo,' greeted Yetunde. 'It's nice to see you although we were not expecting you today.' These days she always avoided the other's direct gaze if she could.

"Good afternoon, Mrs Osaro," replied Sunbo, without her usual gaiety and confidence. 'May I sit down?'

'Please do.'

'I'm sorry to barge in on you like this, knowing how very busy you are, but I have a very personal problem and I'm badly in need of advice. I have always admired your cool and rational way of thinking and dealing with things and with your experience in life I'm sure you'll be able to help me.'

'I'm sorry to hear that you've a problem, Sunbo. In what way can I help you?'

'Well, it's like this. **My marriage is about to break up**.' She paused and stared straight at Yetunde, trying to assess how she was taking the news. The other met the challenge and stared back, her face impassive although her heart was beating fast. *Neat! Here it comes,* she thought. *She's going to accuse me of breaking up her home.*

Sunbo went on quietly. 'Yesterday night, Yinka told me he had fallen in love with another woman but refused to tell me who the lady is. He said I will find out later. I was completely shattered. He and I are very fond of each other. We may have our differences like most couples but we get on very well. I have noticed a certain coolness in our relationship recently. A wife can always tell when her man is having an affair. Anyway, I thought nothing would come out of it, like one or two he has had before.' *Great! She wants me to know that Yinka is a flirt,* Yetunde thought. 'But when he actually told me that he was going to **move out of the house** because he could not go on deceiving the children and me, I decided I must act. I must seek advice. I must **fight for my home**. The children and I love Yinka and we need him. This other woman doesn't. He told me he still loves us but that he must be true to his conscience. That's my Yinka. So noble—nothing underhand about him.' She began to sob.

Yetunde went and placed a hand on her shoulder, trying to calm her. She was at a loss to know what to say.

'I'm er, er, very much surprised by what you've told me. It's a painful experience for a wife to know that her husband is having an affair, and to be told that the marriage is over is even worse. In what way can I help you?'

'Well, Mrs Osaro, I thought perhaps you could advise me as to what to do. Do you think that I'm right to insist on fighting to keep Yinka? Not to accept that he wants to leave the children and me? I really don't know what to do. Plead with him? Tell him to go to hell? I'm hurt and have my pride, but I also love him. I'm confused.'

'Couldn't you discuss the matter with a close friend of the family? A relation, perhaps?'

'No, no,' said Sunbo emphatically. 'Yinka and I never discuss our marital problems with anyone. He would be mad at me if he knew that I've come to you with this problem, so **please don't tell him**.'

'Er, I won't. There would be no point in doing so.'

'Thank you. We normally thrash out ourselves whatever differences there are between us. I decided to come and confide in you because of the nature of the problem.'

'I think the best thing is for you to talk things over with him again. Make him know how much you and the children love and need him.'

'Will it work?'

'It might. At lcast you'll know where you stand. There are no hoops with which a woman can bind a man to her if he has decided to leave her. However, at this moment your husband has probably changed his mind. Forget about pride and have a **heart-to-heart talk** with him.'

'Thank you, Mrs Osaro. I knew you would be sympathetic to my problem.'

Yetunde sat with her head in her hands for some minutes after Sunbo had left. What a mess! She had not been fooled for a moment. She was sure that Sunbo had discovered her affair with her husband and had come to **warn her in a subtle way** that she was not going to give in but was ready to fight to keep her home.

Indeed that was what had happened. Sunbo had always known that her husband was very fond of Mrs Osaro but had thought it harmless as she herself had had a crush on several of her teachers at school. It had all been part of growing up. Lately she had suspected that Yinka was seeing a woman. She had sent out friends to investigate and everyone of them had told her that the lady was Mrs Osaro. She had been shocked. What special attraction did this older woman have for Yinka? She couldn't see it. She was furious and wanted to have it out with her husband, but her sister **Mope** had told her that the publicity would do no-one any good and that there might be nothing in the relationship. She did not think that Yetunde would leave her husband, who had just been promoted **Deputy Secretary in the Ministry**, for Yinka, who although good-looking and well-off, was after all only an **artist**. Yetunde might not be a **gold-digger**, but women generally liked highly placed men, and rumour had it that she and her husband got on quite well. The best course of action, said Mope, was for Sunbo to pretend to take Yetunde into her confidence and tell her Yinka was going to leave his family. This should **jar her conscience** into ending the relationship. Even if the plan backfired and Yetunde told Yinka that his wife had been to see her, it would not matter, it would only precipitate things and Sunbo would know what the situation really was.

Mrs Adebayo had burst into tears when her daughter told her that she had been having an affair with a married man and that the wife had come to accuse her in a subtle manner of breaking up her home.

'You've **disappointed me badly**, Yetunde,' she said, drying her eyes and shaking her head.

'In what way, Mum?' asked the stunned daughter, who had expected at least some sympathy from her mother.

'After the **Christian upbringing** I thought I had successfully given my daughters, I am very disappointed that you, a wife and a mother, should have an affair with a married man or have an affair at all. I see now that I have failed in my duty and may the Good Lord forgive us all.'

'Amen, Mother. But we have really **committed no offence**.'

'Why did you do it? Didn't your vows in the church mean anything to you? Were you just seeking a way of getting your own back at Chibuzor for being unfaithful? **Two wrongs don't make a right**, and besides you've got your **reputation** to think of.'

'I was not trying to get my own back at Chibuzor. I'm really **in love with Yinka**. He's such a wonderful person.'

'All right, you're in love with him, but why did you have to do anything about it? You can admire someone and be friends with him. You didn't have to become lovers. You must **stop seeing him henceforth**.'

'Stop seeing him! That would be difficult to do. It would break both our hearts.'

'Well, let it. It's only a small sacrifice for both of you, when you think of the problems you're creating. Does your husband know?'

'I don't think so.'

'Good. Now is the time to allow **sanity to prevail**. Harden up your heart and stop seeing Yinka, and in a short while the pain will go. You're both trying to break up two good marriages out of pure **lust and selfishness**. I'm surprised that you've not given a thought to the effect on your partners and the children. If people paired off each time they fell in love, the world would be like a great chess board and there would be no marriages left. **Nip this affair in the bud** right away and redeem yourself.'

'But I won't be true to myself. I love Yinka.'

'I don't doubt that, but women tend to be more emotional about these things than men. To him this is probably just **another affair**.'

'I don't think so.'

'Anyway, Yetunde, I know I'm being hard, but you have no right to love him. You're already committed to another man.'

'But I'm not going to leave my family.'

'What do you want? To go on committing **adultery**? Think of the sorrow you've caused Sunbo who has not offended you in any way. Switch all your affection back to **Chibuzor** who loves you. I know you've been going through some strains at home recently and perhaps this relationship with Yinka is a sort of relief. It's always nice for a woman to be wooed, wined, and dined. It's a lovely feeling especially when the couple do not face the strains of everyday living together. If you were married to Yinka, you probably would not still be in love with him. Stop seeing him now. Go and think about it.'

For days Yetunde struggled with her feelings. She felt **cheated and trapped**. All this talk about marital vows, loyalty to husband and children, it was **emotional blackmail**. Why couldn't she go on seeing Yinka if it made her happy to do so? Why must she sacrifice her happiness for others? After all, you only live once. She knew, however, that she had to stop seeing him. Where would the relationship lead them? She could not desert her family and he had not actually decided to leave his yet, no matter what Sunbo wanted her to believe. And the future? Would they continue to feel this way about each other? Something told her she had asked herself this question many years ago when she had just met Chibuzor. Would Yinka not long for the company of younger women when she was a lot less active and attractive than now? How nice it would be to continue this way. But she knew that something was bound to give. If her husband ever discovered the affair he would never forgive her and would seek ways of making life unbearable for her.

At their next meeting Yinka gave her a **bracelet made of coral beads** which he slipped on to her wrist with great ceremony.

'You're my queen,' he told her tenderly, 'and this is a symbol of my **everlasting love** for you. If you ever take it off without my permission, your hand will automatically drop off.' He added, with **mock gravity**, 'At least, so said the **juju man** in my village who had cooked the bracelet for a month in his shrine. It's supposed to make you fall in love with me.'

'Did you have to go to a juju man for that?' she teased.

'Of course. You've proved a most **difficult conquest**.' He winked at her and they laughed.

Throughout the evening she controlled her emotions and tried to behave normally, but how her heart ached when she thought of what she had to tell him before leaving. They went out for a drink and came back to listen to some music. Afterwards, they discussed some of the paintings he had brought to show her.

Later, as they kissed goodnight, she suddenly broke away and said she had something important to tell him. After stumbling for an opening, she **blurted out that they had to stop seeing each other**.

He did not take her seriously at first, but as she sobbed and went about the flat collecting her things, he **went wild**. He pulled her roughly into his arms and held her fast. She struggled and told him he was hurting her. He threatened to **kill both of them** if she left the flat. She was his and he was not going to let her go. He began to drag her towards the bedroom. She was terribly frightened by the look in his eyes. It was as if he had lost his sanity. Was he going to kill her? She mustered all her strength and gave him a push. They both fell down and she cried out in pain as her **elbow hit a chair**. This seemed to bring him to his senses as he quickly got up and went over to her. She pushed him away, struggled to her feet, grabbed her handbag, and **stumbled**

out of the flat. He called after her but she did not stop. She got into her car and drove off trembling.

The next day he rang her but she wouldn't speak to him. Then he sent her a note apologising for the way he had behaved and saying that he could hardly wait to see her the following Thursday. She neither replied to his note nor turned up at the flat. She was not angry with him, although she had been shocked by the way he had reacted to the news of their parting. At worst she had expected him to walk off in a huff, but to turn **violent**! Sunbo had stopped coming to the shop and business between them had ground to a halt. After a few more futile attempts to reach her by phone, Yinka left her alone. Thoughts of him loomed large in her mind but she suppressed the temptation to get in touch with him. Time would heal the wounds. Or would it?

Chapter 5

Nine months later, the Osaros threw a party to celebrate their daughter's **graduation**. It was a moderate affair but everyone was gaily dressed and in a good mood, especially the parents, who intended to announce the **engagement of their daughter to Bode** during the party. Yetunde had taken her mother's advice and had reactivated her affection for her husband. They had taken a long holiday away from home and had returned with some of the **old magic back in their relationship**. She still thought longingly of Yinka and knew that she would never really stop loving him, but she was content with the way things were. Both families were still intact.

She was surprised that evening when she came into the garden to find **Yinka and Sunbo** among the invited guests. Who had invited them? She had not set eyes on either of them since she had left him in the flat.

They were elegantly dressed in **Nigerian attire** and they looked happy. He had his back to her but turned instinctively as she drew near. Her heart ached dully as their eyes met but she wore a bright smile and moved forward to do her hostess stuff.

'Hello, Sunbo, hello Yinka,' she greeted them effusively. 'How nice to see you. It's been a long time. How are the children?'

'Good evening, Mrs Osaro,' said Sunbo, smiling. 'The children are fine. I saw Oghogho at the Kingsway Stores the other day and she told me about this party and later sent us an invitation card.'

'Oh, I see. How's business? Is everything okay?'

'Yes, thank you. You'll have to ask Yinka about the business though. I've stopped working with him at the studio and have gone back to the **bank**.'

'Have you, really? Do you enjoy it?'

'Very much. Now I can practise my profession. Excuse me, please. That's Mrs

Akpan over there. I must go and say "hello" to her.' And with that she left her husband with Yetunde.

Clever girl, thought the latter, *she purposely left us together so as to find out our reaction to each other.*

'So, how are things, Yinka?' she asked, looking into his eyes to find out if he still cared.

'Fine, Yetunde,' he said, smiling faintly, twirling his glass in his hand and looking very much at ease. She was slightly disappointed. She had expected to see him looking **gaunt and miserable**. Where was all his proclaimed 'everlasting love' if he was looking so well and content?

'Er, I see that you now take **alcohol**.'

'Any wonder? You've driven me to drink, so to speak. I get drunk sometimes so as to forget you, but I just can't.'

Now, that was better. He still cared. 'You don't have to do that,' she told him lightly, feeling pleased.

'Do what?'

'Drink yourself silly, I mean.'

'Look, Yetunde, I must see you,' he said urgently, moving closer to her, unconcerned about who was looking at them. She moved back. Out of the corner of her eye she could see Sunbo watching them while pretending to chat with a couple nearby.

'All right, Yinka,' she said, deliberately raising her voice a little. 'I must circulate. There's Sunbo waiting for you over there.' She waved to Sunbo and moved on. She avoided him and his wife for the rest of the evening.

The party was a success and went on until **one o'clock in the morning**, when the crowd began to thin out, and by one-thirty the last of the guests had gone. Chibuzor left to take home some relatives who had no transport of their own and Yetunde went into the sitting room to fix herself a drink. She was tired but happy, although the reappearance of Yinka had almost spoilt her evening. She pushed thoughts of him aside and thought about the future. There was a faraway look in her eyes. Her daughter would get married the following year and perhaps within a year or two she would be made a **grandmother**. That would be nice! A real trendy one she would be. As the youngest child in the family would be at college then, she and Chibuzor would at last be able to see the world as they had planned. Each year they would go to a different city—**Sydney, Tokyo, Peking, Istanbul, Paris**. It would be such fun! How lovely it would have been if she could have gone on these trips with Yinka who admired things the way she did. Her husband never saw deeper than the surface. He was always impatient with her if she stopped to admire the scenery or a piece of artwork. He said it was **potty** to stand and stare at an object like a cow. People would think she was an **imbecile**.

Now, Yinka shared her sentiments in such matters. If only there was a way in which...

'Yetunde,' whispered someone behind her. She was startled and dropped her glass.

Yinka had come up stealthily behind her. 'I just had to come back and see you,' he said in a **husky voice**. 'I've missed you badly these past months. Don't you see we were meant for each other?' He took her in his arms and began to murmur words of endearment. She was too **stupefied** to resist. She still cared for him but this was crazy.

'Mummy, are you all right?' called out **Oghogho**, coming barefoot down the stairs, pulling on her housecoat. 'Oh, sorry,' she cried, on seeing the couple in each other's arms. She turned and ran back up the stairs and **banged her door**.

Yetunde pushed Yinka away, ready to go after her. 'See what you've done? Please leave immediately. I don't ever want to set eyes on you again. I know you'll only bring trouble.' As she turned to go upstairs, she noticed her husband at the door leading to the garden. How long had he been there? Suddenly, a **mad gleam** came into his eyes and he rushed at Yinka, giving him a blow on the jaw. The latter, glad at last of an opportunity to hurt his rival physically, sprang back, took off his agbada and they began to **fight**.

Yetunde was disgusted at the sight. What were they fighting about? She shouted at them to stop but no-one paid her any attention. She felt helpless and called out to her daughter. When there was no response, she went and tried the door to her room. It was locked and there was no sound from within. She became alarmed and rushed down to fetch her husband who was still fighting with Yinka.

'Stop, stop, both of you,' she screamed at them, trying to pull them apart. They stopped. 'How silly! Two grown men fighting like children, over nothing! Chibuzor,' she continued, leading him away, 'Oghogho has locked herself up in her room and won't open the door to me. Come and tell her to.'

"Leave her alone,' said the other. 'What did you expect? That she should give you a pat on the back for what she saw?'

'Don't be silly. What did she see?'

'What I saw—**you in your lover's arms**.'

'Nonsense! Have you asked me for explanations? Look, come and persuade her to open up. She might be doing herself some harm. You know what a sensitive girl she is.'

They both went upstairs and, when Oghogho would not open the door, Chibuzor put his weight to it. It would not yield. He banged on it, calling out to her. When there was no response he became alarmed himself and told his wife to fetch Udoh.

'Here, let me help,' offered a sober Yinka, coming up the stairs, wiping blood from his lips.

'You, you **louse**,' began Chibuzor, rushing angrily towards him. 'You're still here?' He controlled himself and said in a lower voice, 'Please **get out of my house immediately**.'

Yinka turned and walked out of the house.

They found Oghogho **unconscious**, a half-empty bottle of **sleeping pills** by her. Yetunde screamed and fainted. Both women were rushed to the nearest private hospital where a doctor successfully **pumped out the contents of Oghogho's stomach**. When she woke up she was surprised to find her father by her hospital bed. Then she remembered what had happened and she asked for her mother.

'She's er, er, resting at home,' said her father.

'Really?' she asked incredulously. Has her mother lost interest in her family? Previously, you could never keep her away when any of her children was ill, and it did not matter if she herself was desperately ill.

'Er,' continued her father, 'the shock of what happened was too much for her and she's a bit weak. The doctor told her to rest.'

'Oh, I see. Who's looking after her at home then? Have you told Grandma?'

'No. The old people should not be bothered. Udoh is there and she should be all right in a few days.'

'Good. When do I go home? What did the doctor say?'

'He wants to observe you for two days. Bode was here this afternoon. He's coming back later in the evening after work. I left the office early to be with you.'

'Thank you, Dad. I'd like to see Mum. Isn't she well enough to visit me this evening?'

'I'll find out.'

Yetunde had come to the hospital and had begun crying and blaming herself for what had happened that evening. Chibuzor did not say a word to her, but hung around until they were both told by the doctor that their daughter was **out of danger**, and was asleep. She wanted to stay at the hospital but he would not let her. She was amazed at his behaviour but kept calm.

When they got home he told her to **move her things from the bedroom into one of**

the guest rooms, as he could not sleep in the same room with her after what had happened. She refused. How could she live in the guest room in her own home?

'I see you're going to be difficult. One would have expected you would be so ashamed of yourself that you would accept any decision I made.'

'How can you make a decision when you've not asked me what it was all about?'

'Ask what? I was witness to the disgraceful scene. You, a married woman, had the **impudence** to invite your lover to the matrimonial home and there proceed to indulge in love play in full view of your husband and daughter. How humiliating for your family and what a dazzling example for your daughter on the night of her engagement. It certainly calls for an encore.' He gave a bitter laugh.

'But Chi, it wasn't what you thought at all. Let me explain.'

'Please spare me the whole sordid story. What do you want to explain? That you found him so **virile** that you fell in love with him? What did you see in a **cheap artist** who cannot earn a living without splashing paint about? What education did he have? I only tolerated his company because you did business with him. He's far below the level of people I socialise with. To think that we shared the same woman! Not a girlfriend, mind you. My wife! A lady I've loved and respected all my life! The mother of my children! And this **unsavoury adultery** of yours almost cost us the life of our daughter.'

She began to cry.

'You'll not go unpunished. You have one of two options. You can move right away into the spare room and we can keep up the pretense of being man and wife, although any closeness between us will be non-existent. That does not mean that you can turn yourself into a **whore**. You'll sell your share of the art shop and be a **full-time housewife**, going out only with my permission.'

She was dry-eyed now as she listened, horrified by the **venom** in his voice. She tried to make light of it. 'You can't be serious, Chi. How can I live like that? What explanations do I give the children?'

'Look, Yetunde,' he said, going to her and wagging a finger at her. 'You keep the children out of this. If you drag them in, I shall murder you, and I've never laid a finger on you before. Now, I've told Oghogho that what she saw didn't mean a thing and that **Yinka was very drunk** last night. I don't know if she's accepted that, but she's not at all keen to see you and I'm warning you to **keep away from the hospital** as the sight of you might worsen her condition. I did my utmost to convince the doctor that she had been depressed of late and probably took an overdose due to forgetfulness. It could be a case for the police if the truth came out. A most disgraceful affair.'

'Did you say Oghogho didn't want to see me?'

'She didn't actually say so, but that was the impression I got. Mercifully, the boys are away so they never need to know what a **tramp** their mother is, if you behave yourself well.'

'Chi, what are you saying? Nothing happened that evening although...'

'Hush! I don't want to know. The other option is that you **pack your things and quietly leave and go away**, at least for a while, until I've worked out the details about when you may see the children. Oghogho and Efe are old enough to make their own decisions but if you insist on trying to justify your actions to them, then I'll make them see the **enormity of your crime** and by the time I finish my story they'll never want to have anything to do with you again.'

She believed him. Whenever he chose to give his own version of a quarrel he had **total disregard for the truth**, and he would speak so convincingly that the listener would be in no doubt as to the guilt of the other party. She felt **trapped** and weighed down by guilt. If Oghogho had not been involved in any way, she would have told him where to get off, but if the girl had died...

'I want you to choose now,' said Chibuzor. 'Everything must be settled before the children come home.'

There was silence as she thought of what decision to make.

'I'll go,' she said sadly. 'Yes, I think I'll go.'

'You'll **desert your children**?' He was shocked, for much as he wanted to see her suffer for what she had done, he wanted the family together. His affection for her had momentarily turned to hate, but they had been together for more than twenty years, most of which had been happy ones.

'I'm not deserting my children, Chi,' she said quietly. 'You're sending me away without even giving me a chance to explain what led to the incident you saw.'

'I don't want to know,' he said stubbornly.

'However,' continued Yetunde wearily, 'I cannot live like a stranger in my own home and keep up the pretence that everything is normal between us. If that's all the future now holds for us, then I'll go.'

'Fine, fine, fine, if that's what you want,' he said, working himself up again. 'I would have thought that, as a mother, staying close to your children at any cost would be worth it.'

'Not on the conditions you give,' she replied.

'I see. After what you've done, how do you expect to be treated?' He would like to have her near him so that he could see at close quarters how effective the punishment was. Now, she was going to escape... He sought feverishly for other ways of torturing her but could find none at that moment.

'All right, go. I'll contact you later.'

'What about **money**?'

'What money?'

'The money in our **joint account**. Let's find out how much is left in it and decide what I should have.'

'That account will be **frozen**. I'm not touching it either. The money will be used for the children as the need arises.'

'But I've no personal account like you have. All I've been earning went in there. I don't mind if the money is kept for the children but I need something now. How do I pay for accommodation and other things?'

'You have a business,' he pointed out.

'Yes, but no cash in hand. Every **kobo** I own is in that joint account. I think you're being unreasonably cruel.'

'So! Apart from committing adultery, breaking up your home, driving your daughter to suicide, you don't want to provide for your children? Hm, how strange! You're totally **selfish**, Yetunde.'

Every word he uttered hurt and she began to cry again.

'You're cruel, cruel, cruel,' she screamed at him. 'What shall I do? Yesterday I had a roof over my head, today I'm **homeless**.'

'The decision is yours.' He was beginning to feel better now that she was distraught. *"You're in for a lot more unhappiness. Wait until I gradually start turning the children against you,"* he said silently. He would never forgive her.

'When I caught you with a woman last year,' she began, 'I forgave you and...'

'I don't know what you're talking about,' he cut in rudely. 'Please leave.'

She left and checked in at a **hotel**. She could not go to her mother and face further condemnation and she could not impose on friends. The **scandal**! Chi was right, it was best to keep everything quiet. What about the children? Did Oghogho really not want to see her? Couldn't she call at the hospital and explain things to her? How embarrassing! The more she thought about it the less she liked the idea. It was best to **let sleeping dogs lie**. And when the boys came on holiday? A lump came into her throat. Well, they would all have to adjust to the new situation. Of one thing she was sure—there was no way she could share the same roof as her husband after his **shocking display of cruelty and hypocrisy**!

Some days afterwards, she phoned him for news of Oghogho and he told her she had left for **Ondo State** where she was going to do her **National Youth Service** for nine months.

When she went back to the shop, she found that **Inyang** had been having her troubles too. Her husband, who had been seriously ill for some time, had suffered a **stroke**, and she was accompanying him abroad for treatment. They did not have much hope for his recovery, but anything was worth trying. Yetunde forgot her problems for a minute at the news. Poor Inyang! She always went to pieces whenever any member of her family was ill, and this had certainly affected her deeply. She looked so **haggard and tense**. They were going to be away for at least six months.

Yetunde was glad to combine Inyang's duties with hers, as she became so busy that she **wallowed less in remorse and self-pity**. She wrote as usual to the boys without giving a hint of what had taken place. Oghogho, on the other hand, wrote only after two months to say she was glad to note that her mother was back from the **health institution** to which she had been confined and that she hoped she was now very well. She was puzzled by the content of the letter, but thought no further of it.

When Yinka Taiwo left the Osaros that night he had parked his car down the road and had seen Oghogho being carried out of the house. He was **visibly shaken** and terribly sorry for the trouble he had caused the family. If the girl should die he would never forgive himself. He could not understand the impulse that had made him come back that night, after keeping away from Yetunde for more than ten months. He had not particularly wanted to attend the party but Oghogho had personally delivered the invitation card to him with a cheery, 'Auntie, Uncle, you must come. It's going to be my big night.' And it had been, too. She looked so **radiant and happy**. He sincerely hoped she would be all right. She was such a likeable girl.

He decided there and then to **steer clear of the family**. Not that Yetunde would be anxious to see him anyway. She had always said that he would bring trouble, and he had.

After the party, Sunbo came to the conclusion that her husband could never overcome his **infatuation** for Mrs. Osaro even though she was convinced that they had stopped seeing each other. Friends had told her not to worry but she was an impatient lady who hated harbouring feelings of **insecurity** about anything.

Over the next few months, he would disappear for a day or two. He called it his **'withdrawal'**. He said he needed to think and get inspiration for new work. She did not believe him. He must be still **'mooning'** over his 'old woman'. He still treated her well but as she knew that his heart was no longer in the home, she did not want to hang around. She would have to set up a proper home for herself and their four children as his 'withdrawals' became more and more frequent and began to get on her nerves.

She was, however, not going to make things easy for him. He spent less time in the studio now and their booming interior decoration business was declining and his boys began to leave. He had to reduce her **housekeeping money**. *Now's the time to beat it*, she told herself. She got a place off **Isolo Expressway** and gradually moved her light valuables there without his noticing anything amiss.

One night when he was off on yet another 'withdrawal' she threw a lighted matchstick carelessly in a corner where **alcohol was stored**. In no time the whole place was up in flames and she rushed out of the house with the children to raise the alarm at a neighbour's.

'Help, help, fire, fire,' she cried, banging on the door.

By the time the firemen arrived, the flat and the studio were **razed to the ground**. The tears flowed freely and there was sympathy from every side.

'Poor woman! She has lost everything she's worked for in her life.'

'Never mind, at least no lives were lost.'

'Lucky thing she's a light sleeper, otherwise it would have been a different story.'

'Where was the husband?'

'Out.'

'At this time of the night? Leaving his family all alone?'

'What a shock he'll get when he returns.'

'Serves him right.'

Sunbo went to camp temporarily with her married sister while she waited for Yinka to contact her. He raced there some days later when he discovered the disaster. He embraced his wife and children and was on the verge of tears.

'Everything was lost,' wailed Sunbo. It was easy to feign tears. 'What shall we do, Yinka? Where will we get the money to re-establish? We'll die in poverty.'

'Don't worry, darling,' he comforted her. 'The important thing is that you and the children are safe. Everything was **insured**. We'll collect the money and start again. We're still young enough for that.'

'Oh good,' enthused his wife, although she had other ideas.

When he went to his insurance company he was told that the policy had **expired** a few days before the fire and, as the company was not liable at the time, there was nothing to pay. They were sympathetic but there was nothing they could do as a reminder had been sent to him. He remembered vaguely receiving such a letter. He felt like **suicide**. So, all was indeed lost!

Sunbo collapsed into a chair when she heard. To please her, he took out what little money he had left in his account and told her to go looking for accommodation. She took the money and a few weeks later told him she had found a place for herself and the children and that for her the **marriage was over** as she could not face another stretch of being **'grass widow'**. She told him she knew what had been going on all along and blamed him for the disaster he had brought on the family.

He was stunned by her decision but did nothing to persuade her to change her mind. She might cool down later and they could get back together. If the separation was final, well, perhaps it was for the best.

Chapter 6

There was a **chilly atmosphere** the first time the children visited Yetunde, as they sat on the edges of their chairs and watched her as if she were a stranger. Not even lunch and discussions about their studies and friends put them at ease. She had not expected all to be plain sailing at this initial stage of the change in their family life, but this was disappointing. Later, when they all called at her mother's, they were their usual buoyant selves as they roamed the house and chatted with their grandmother. Back at her place in the evening, they each gave her an impersonal peck on the cheek, got into their father's car and Efe roared off. It was as if they could not get away from her fast enough. Were they **blaming her for breaking up the home**? She hoped Chibuzor had not broken his word and given them a malicious account of the incident that led to her leaving. She had kept her promise and had said nothing to them about it, but she was now having second thoughts. Since the boys had not been around at the time, perhaps it was best not to go into details with them, but **Oghogho should know the facts**. She was a woman now and shortly to be married herself. Yetunde made up her mind to have a heart-to-heart talk with her daughter the next time she came to Lagos.

Mr. Akpan never recovered from his illness. He **died in a London hospital** a year later, and his wife brought his corpse home to **Cross River State** for burial. When her period of mourning was over, she told Yetunde that she would like to sell her share of their business as she had decided to settle in **Calabar** and run a gift shop in one of the international hotels there.

Yetunde wished she had the money to buy out Inyang's share, as a new partner might pose some problems. She would just have to persuade her bank to give her another loan, and she would get a capable assistant to do some of the running around so that she could have more time to relax. She would like to go away on holiday with the children more frequently before they began to lead their own lives. As it was, she missed their company a lot. Chibuzor had **refused to let the two younger ones spend their holiday with her**. This was unacceptable to her and she contacted a lawyer who advised that there was no need to go to court to fight for the custody of children of thirteen and fifteen who were away at boarding schools for most of the year anyway. As he saw it, they had already left home and the choice of where they spent their holidays should be left to them. They needn't go to their father if they didn't want to. On reflection she agreed that perhaps the boys did prefer going to their father at the moment. She would have to be patient and wait until they drew closer to her again.

After completing her **National Youth Service**, Oghogho came back to Lagos to look for a job.

She had gradually become more relaxed towards her mother, although she fended her off each time the latter wanted to have any serious discussion with her.

'Relax, Mum, don't worry,' she would tell her solicitously. 'You must not get upset. You might have a **relapse**.'

'A relapse from what?' Yetunde had to ask impatiently one day. 'Oghogho, what are you talking about?'

'Er, well, Dad did say that any mention of last year's incident was likely to start you off again.'

'But I want to talk about it. It seems silly to pretend that nothing happened. You're grown-up enough now to understand situations like that and draw your own conclusions. What did your father say was likely to start off again?'

'Your **illness**.'

'What illness?' she asked bewildered. 'I don't have any major illness.'

'Dad said you had a **mental breakdown** soon after the incident and you had to be taken away and confined to an **institution**.'

Yetunde was **dumbfounded**. How could Chi be so wicked!

'Did he say that I was **mad**?'

'He said you had to be handled with care and that no reference should be made to the incident or it might trigger the illness, and that there's really no definite cure.'

'Did he tell the boys that too?'

'Yes. He explained that that was why they could not come to stay with you while on holiday. He said that you might appear normal to us, but the doctor said that you're **no longer fit enough to be entrusted with children**.'

'Heavens! I think your father has **overplayed his hand** this time! He told me not to refer to the incident so as not to upset you, and then he went round to tell you damaging lies about me. Look, Oghogho, I'm not mad and never was at any time. Ask your father to give you the name of the institution to which he claimed I was confined. If I was ever taken away, your granny, Udoh and nanny would know about it. You can talk to them. I will **never forgive your father for this**.'

'Please, Mum, take it calmly. It was wrong of Dad to have invented such a story, but don't let it lead to another major quarrel. It would upset us very much. Already we don't know which direction to turn.'

'I now understand why you all kept me at **arm's length**. A mental case! I'll decide what to do later. Meanwhile this was what led to the scene you witnessed after the party. I'll put the facts plainly to you and hope that you'll understand why I could not accept the conditions your father gave me. I'm sure he did not tell you about them.'

'No, he didn't,' said Oghogho, beginning to see another side of her father she had not suspected. She felt miserable and confused after her mother had narrated her story.

'Forgive me, Mum,' she cried, putting her arms around her mother. 'I feel partly responsible for what happened.'

'You? In what way?'

'When I took the invitation card for my party to Auntie Sunbo and Uncle Yinka, he was not keen on attending and he was going to make excuses, but as I'm very fond of them I told him that I would be **extremely disappointed if they failed to turn up**. Auntie Sunbo then promised that they would come even if they had to cancel other engagements. If I had not insisted, they wouldn't have come and what took place afterwards would not have taken place. I've contributed to **two broken homes**.' She began to sob.

'Don't cry, Oghogho. It's all in the past. Did you say two broken homes?'

'Yes. Ours and Uncle Yinka's.'

'Has his marriage broken up? I heard about a fire which destroyed all they possessed. Did they break up after that?'

'Yes, Auntie Sunbo told me when I went for
an interview at the bank where she works.
She's expecting a baby from someone else.
She looked well and quite happy.'

'Hm! **Lucky girl**!'

'She said Uncle Yinka is trying to start all
over again but is finding it tough.
Apparently the insurance policy on their
property had expired at the time of the fire,
so they were left penniless. I saw him in
traffic last week and he was looking a bit
shabby and worn out. It's a pity.'

Yetunde was sorry to hear about his
misfortune but said nothing.

'Are you still fond of Uncle Yinka, Mum?'
asked Oghogho suddenly.

Her mother turned away. 'I don't think so,'
she said, but her **voice gave her away**.

'What about Dad?'

'I'm fond of your father even though I've
just realised what a **cruel, vindictive man**
he is. He's made me suffer unnecessarily

and almost ruined the good relationship between me and my children. Why wouldn't he listen to my explanation and forgive if there's anything to forgive? He simply threw me out without a kobo. I don't condone unfaithfulness in a marriage, particularly when it's been a happy one, but whatever the case there should always be room for forgiveness if the guilty party is repentant. In this case nothing was going on at the time he thought there was, but he wouldn't even listen. I didn't make a song and a dance out of it two years ago when I caught him with a...'

'...Woman in a **guest house in Surulere**.'

'You, you know about it?' asked her mother in surprise.

'Bode and I saw him although he doesn't know we did.'

'Well, well, well! You didn't tell me about it.'

'I couldn't have. I was **protecting the home**. That was why last year's incident affected me the way it did. I couldn't take it and didn't stop to think. I'm sorry, Mum.'

'That's all right. I probably would have done the same too.'

She felt relieved now that all was out. If the girl realised what a **hypocrite** her father was, there was no more need to go and fight him at home that evening as she had intended to do.

A week after her talk with Oghogho, Yinka phoned her at the shop to invite himself to her flat.

'Are you still very angry with me?' he asked when she kept silent.

Was she? She searched her heart.

'No.'

'Is there any reason why we shouldn't meet?'

'No.'

'See you at five tomorrow.'

He had certainly **fallen upon bad times**. He had aged considerably and was looking a bit **unkempt**, but he was in high spirits as he kissed her lightly on the cheek.

The evening had none of the previous intimacy between them as they talked about their work and friends. He lived in 'their flat' and used one of the rooms as his studio. Thanks to some good contracts he was able to secure, business was beginning to take off and he hoped shortly to be able to afford a bigger place. Meanwhile he had to work very hard to pay **maintenance for his children**.

Soon, they were meeting regularly again.

'Let's **live together**,' he suggested.

'No way,' she told him. 'It's more fun like this, both of us enjoying a certain amount of **freedom**.

'But I would like to sleep with you, wake up with you, and...'

'Me too, but after more than twenty years of doing that with a man, I need a break. **Later perhaps**.'

He had to be content with that but he was sure she would change her mind. Women always liked to get married as it gave them a sense of security and respectability.

'Oghogho, now that we're friends again there's something unpleasant I have to tell you,' said Yinka to her one day when she and Bode called at his studio. The latter was in an adjoining room examining some artwork.

'What is it, Uncle?' she asked.

'I think it was **extremely foolish** of you to attempt to take your own life just because you saw something you found disagreeable to you. As you discovered, your death would have been a waste of time as it would not have solved whatever problems there were. You can't **blackmail couples into staying together** if they don't want to. In future, steer clear of such emotional involvement.

Learn to accept things you cannot help. We all want you alive.'

'Precisely what I told her myself, Uncle,' said Bode, coming into the room. 'I was very disappointed by her action. If I have to rush her to the hospital each time there's a minor crisis in the home, the strain of it all would make her a widow in no time.'

'Don't rub it in, Bode,' she said, ashamed of herself. 'I promised you and Granny last year that I would never behave like that again, and I intend to keep my promise.'

'Good girl!' chorused both men.

'Is that Madam?' asked a voice over the telephone early one Sunday morning.

'Yes, who's that?' asked Yetunde.

'It's me, Ma.'

'Oh, **Udoh**,' she said, recognising the voice. 'I hope there's nothing wrong. Is any of the boys home?'

'No, Ma. It's master. He don **collapse for bath-room** and he no fit get up. Nanny dey wif am. Wetin make I do?' (In standard English: 'No, Ma. It's master. He has collapsed in the bathroom and he can't get up. Nanny is with him. What should I do?')

'Call his doctor quickly, Udoh.'

'Which doctor?'

'Eh, hold on.' Had Chibuzor changed doctors? 'Oghogho, wake up,' she called out to her daughter who was there for the weekend. 'Udoh's on the phone. Your father has collapsed in the bathroom. Who's his doctor now? Is it still Dr. Twangi?'

'I think so. I don't really know. He's hardly ever ill.'

'Well, he is now. Okay, I'll tell Udoh to ring him up. I remember his number.' Back on the phone, Udoh was in a panic.

'Madam, come quick o. Nanny say e be like say master no dey breathe again. Come o Madam, I take God beg you.' (In standard English: 'Madam, come quickly. Nanny says it seems master is not breathing again. Come, Madam, I beg you in God's name.')

Yetunde and Oghogho flung on their clothes and drove at once to **Ikoyi**. Chibuzor was quickly taken to the **General Hospital**, was examined and rushed to the theatre for an operation. Yetunde rang up two doctor friends who rallied round immediately.

'I should leave him to his fate and go home,' she told herself. 'After all he has done to me, he does not deserve my sympathy. I should go.' But she couldn't. Instead, she was as distressed as Oghogho who kept sobbing. She kept praying that he would not die.

'Don't worry,' the doctor told her some agonising hours later. 'He'll pull through easily. Your old man's as **strong as an ox**.'

He pulled through all right but he needed **intensive care** while recuperating, and she gave up work temporarily to stay with him most of the time and nurse him back to health. She made a point, however, of going back to her flat every night.

He was very pleased to have her near him again and he **feigned weakness** to make her stay longer. He was not sure whether he still loved her or was simply enjoying being looked after by her; still, it was nice to be made so much fuss of.

One night after she had given him his medicine and was leaving, he pulled her to him and kissed her. 'Don't go, Yetunde, stay with me. I think we're still sufficiently fond of each other to live together once more and be a **complete family**. Move back in. What do you say?'

He had taken her completely unawares by his request and she was at a loss for words.

'Oh, er, er, I don't know, Chi,' she replied, sitting on the bed and parting his beard. 'I'll think about it.' Two days later she told him she would come back to him.

Yinka was not surprised at the news; he had been half expecting it for he knew that nursing a convalescent husband was bound to draw out the **protective instinct** in any woman.

'You know how I feel about you,' she tried to soothe him over the phone, 'but, you see, he needs my help and the children would be extremely happy to have their parents together again.'

'I understand, Yetunde,' he said.

Oghogho was very surprised by her mother's decision.

'Is that what you want, Mum?' she asked, as they were packing up at the flat.

Yetunde was taken aback. She looked at her daughter curiously.

'Yes. Why? You don't look pleased.'

'I'm pleased, Mum, very pleased indeed. I love both you and Dad and my dearest wish would be to see you back in the house; but **only if that's what you really want**. Think of yourself, Mum, and whatever your decision is, let it be for yourself, not for Dad and not for us children. It's your life to do what you like with. After all, my brothers and I are not going to live at home for ever.'

The mother pondered. The girl was right! Did she want to go back for herself or for

Chibuzor and the children? Would she be happy?

'I'm sorry, Mum,' apologised Oghogho. 'I see I've got myself involved again. Uncle Yinka and Bode had advised me that it was best to let people sort out their problems themselves. Don't be angry with me.'

'I'm not angry with you at all, darling. You're a very sensible girl, and I'm grateful to you for your **sound advice**. Rest assured that whatever decision I make will be **for myself**. Thank you.'

The next day she rearranged her things and rang to **cancel the order for a removal van**. When she told her husband she was no longer moving back in he was angry.

'You're not? You're **deserting me** when I'm helpless and on my sick bed?'

'I'm not deserting you, Chi, and you're not an invalid. You're much better now and the doctor said you could go back to work next week. However, for the past six weeks I've given up everything else to look after you despite the **campaign of hate** you carried out against me with the children. Your cruelty almost ruined my life.'

'So, now you're having your **revenge**?'

'No. I wouldn't be here if I were. I simply know that I cannot live with you again and be happy, and I certainly do want to be happy. **Pretence would be no use**. We'll remain friends of course and contact each other regularly.'

'Don't bother since you've made up your mind to leave me to die. Don't attend my funeral either if it would be distasteful to you.'

'Stop being **over-dramatic**,' she chided. 'You're perfectly capable of managing your own life and you have a nanny and Udoh to look after you.'

'That notwithstanding, I still need care.'

She was tired of arguing. 'So long,' she said, and went out quietly. She now knew what she wanted.

'I've been waiting and was prepared to wait a long time for you to come to me,' Yinka told her as soon as she stepped into their flat. 'I knew you would come because we **belong together**. You're mine for good.'

She thought: *'We belong together? Sure! Yours for good? I don't know about that! I cherish my* **independence** *and I intend to hang on to it.'*